THE E*PISSED*TEMOLOGIST

By
John-Paul Tarser

The E*pissed*temologist
First Edition
Published by DreamStar Books, November 2004

Lasyard House
Underhill Street
Bridgnorth
Shropshire
WV16 4BB
Tel: 00 870 777 3339
e-mail: dreamstar@jakarna.co.uk

Set in 'Garamond'

Printed and bound in Great Britain by Antony Rowe Ltd

Acknowledgements

I would like to thank Chris Sawyer of *Authors' Aid* who read the manuscript and encouraged me to get it published. Thanks also to Pearson Education / Penguin books for allowing me to quote from Jean-Paul Sartre's novel *Nausea*. Special thanks go to Carlsberg for their 'Special Brew' without which there would be no '*epissed*temology' and no book.

About the author

At the age of 22, the author left a boring office job to become a student. A few months into his course he began to experience attacks of nausea during lectures. He had to force himself to keep going. At this time he read Sartre's novel *Nausea*, to see if this could explain his own. This was the start of a long search for meaning, truth, authenticity and peace of mind.

This book is a send up of his 'search' as well as being a bit of a parody of Sartre's serious philosophy.

Sometime in October

I've got to write everything down, everything that happens from now on, and right now I'm looking at that suitcase in front of me, sitting on the bed like a fat unwanted orphan in this tatty, crappy room.

A familiar feeling of pointlessness descends upon me. How beginnings always seem like endings! I never was any good with holidays, birthdays and the rare 'date'. There's something oddly sad about happiness. On the other hand, I've always found funerals to be uplifting! Like everyone on a collision course for thirty, I've often wondered if I'm a bit bonkers. If I am, I don't think I'm dangerous to anyone. I'm fairly harmless having never broken any major laws nor contributed anything of any worth to anyone.

Like many a sexually unsuccessful adolescent, I became a deep thinker- a face-saving strategy used to convince myself that I was better than my bonking contemporaries. Trouble is, the deeper I thought, the worse I felt, as my increasing self-knowledge did not tell a pretty story. I became a gardener of my own mind, salting the slugs and pulling out the weeds, hoping to find something like tranquillity eventually, but the weeds and slugs just grew back all the stronger. I flirted with religion but never even got a snog; it all seemed so obviously untrue. I still think that Buddhism offers something though, but keep a safe distance in case it lets me down like all the others.

And now this, my first day as a philosophy student, feeling such a fraud! How did I get here? I'm so determined not to have a career that I'm willing to spend three years proving it to myself. But why should I want a career? Ambition is a word that sticks in my throat - it's like an obscenity! A word used by happy, half dead robots that never feel anything negative, that feel the world of commerce and industry offers excitement and a 'challenge'. I've tried all that stuff. It's crap.

The orphan remains on the bed. I'm just stuck in this chair, looking at the walls around me and the bits of *Blue Tack* that still cling to them. They held up the last student's ideas and tastes but now they've all been torn down to leave this bareness, a reflection of my life and mind at the moment. These walls won't get a poster out of me!

Okay! Shall we get it over with good and quickly! I'm 25 years old, a refugee from the world of work. I've got untidy black hair, neither too long nor too short to be mistaken for a fashion statement. My nostrils, earlobes, eyebrows and belly button are defiantly free from gold rings or studs and my face does not sport a silly little pencil beard. This is probably one reason why I'm considered a bit of a weirdo. I'm a non-conformist by not conforming to the trends of the non-conformists. I am what they are *not* and I find my identity in negativity and negation. Not the perfect topic of discussion on dates with young ladies, hence the lack of love and sex in my life. Not that I'm a virgin! Believe me! I met this crazy woman some years ago who dumped me, but I don't want to go into that just yet. All in good time. The priority is to unpack.

I can hear confident laughter and shrill female voices. I can hear, just by their voices, that they've got beautiful big breasts and perfect arses. The thought of meeting them fills me with both excitement and dread. It's like I've got a label on my forehead declaring to the world that I'm a wanker. And I know that as soon as I see them, they will all get a part in my sexual fantasies and I'll wonder if somehow they will be able to read my mind and know what goes on in there. If I don't introduce myself soon, though, I'll be labelled, categorised and avoided so in a minute I'll have to open the door and act all casual, as if I was just going to the toilet or something.

"Hello there. I'm Nicola. I'm opposite you," said a smiling voice when I eventually made my move into the awkward world of social interaction. My brain automatically ran a film in fast motion, a sort of dimly lit soft porn film. It always happens! She radiated 'niceness' and it was almost certain that she had liked ponies when she was just a few years younger. I liked her.

"I'm Antoine," I said, shaking her small hand. "Don't laugh!"

Now, at this point you are probably wondering why such a run-of-the-mill bloke from the South East of England has got such a daft name. It was my mum, you see. She told me that when she was pregnant with me she'd been engrossed in a romantic novel where the hero was called Antoine and she made the decision to name me after him. That was tempting fate, of course! Predictably, the hero and I didn't turn out to share too many characteristics. The Antoine of the novel wasn't in need of the *Alexander technique* for standing up straight, didn't wash with *Biactol* every morning because ordinary soap aggravated his acne, and was certainly not embarrassed by his blocked sinuses.

Whereas the heroic Antoine had women falling at his feet every other chapter, the only woman that ever fell at *this* Antoine's feet was unconscious with drink. This was a swoon brought about by too much vodka at a friend's birthday party I went to. It seems like a million years ago now! Anyway, I'll tell you about it, if you like... I had been chatting her up for a good half an hour and thinking that just maybe that mysterious force between males and females might make itself known and carry us off in an uncontrollable passion of copulation. It was not to be! All of a sudden she slid down the wall and crumpled elegantly to the floor. When I saw her two weeks later, not only did she not recall any of our conversation, she didn't even recognise me. It was then when I began to feel how futile a lot of our efforts are in life. Some of us are dealt a shit hand and are not destined to become heroes, it seems.

This introduction thing continued for a while. I soon found out who was studying what, what 'A' levels had been done and what part of Britain they had all come from. John, for example, wore dark glasses even though the lighting was fine throughout the building. I thought for a moment that he might have been blind, but soon realised that he was just being 'cool' and enigmatic. (Designer or 'off the peg' enigma available in most good stores). His hair was somewhat unusual too. Being a mature student puts you out of touch a bit! I thought he must have fallen over in a paint factory, but again his hair was intentionally as it was - all spiky and shimmering with various alarming hues. Like with my acne, I have always thought that if something invites staring, you were supposed to do the opposite and pretend you hadn't noticed. But I'm not sure that the same applies in this situation. Perhaps I should have said, "Like the hair!" or something like that.... Short hair, long hair, spiky hair, colourful hair, very little hair, no hair, ponytails... I know there's some sort of vocabulary here but I'm damned if I can understand the bloody lingo!

I met several others on my corridor and found them fairly harmless. I liked them, so I'm not always a miserable sod! Perhaps I'll make a go of this, become a great philosopher and write impressive books. Perhaps my future will be more than building society repayments. Perhaps! Amazing things do happen sometimes, don't they?

Eventually, I did manage to put all my stuff away. It was an interesting experience, believe it or not. I watched my hands moving around, twisting about, grasping and moulding themselves around shoes, socks, *Sony Walkman*, pencil cases and so on. I thought about all those tiny muscles expanding and contracting, creating an infinite amount of shapes and pressures that enabled me to grasp anything I wanted. I am the end result of millions of years of evolution - millions of years to pick up socks and put them away! I owe the process so much more, or is it me who's owed? It makes no difference I suppose. Happiness is what's important, isn't it? It doesn't matter what the truth is, as long as you're happy. That's right isn't it? I just don't know. That's what I'm here to find out, I think.

What's important at the moment is that you form a good mental impression of me, seeing I'm the central character. But I find it really embarrassing to talk about myself in any great depth, I'm afraid. You see, I'm one of those people who can't stand having his photo taken, especially in a group. I hate all those cheesy grins and mine always looks the most false. I tend to avoid looking at and describing myself, but I don't want you to think that I'm a bloody monster! I'm not. It's just this 'self consciousness' thing that I have. I have 'self consciousness' in the sense of being 'conscious of a self' and how odd it is to have one. My existence has always felt strange to me and other people don't seem to know what the hell I'm talking about.

I've always felt it odd, for example, that I can raise my arm. When I was at school, I said to my friend: "Isn't it funny that you can raise your arm?" You should have seen the look he gave me! I've seen that look on children when they are absorbed in some gleeful act of sadism - like pulling the wings off flies. He told the whole class and they were soon all laughing at me. I remember being close to tears and shouting back at them.

"All right then! If you're so clever! How do your thoughts get into your muscles?"

They laughed all the more and made me cry, but I also knew at that moment that they didn't understand the question. I still wonder about this question but nowadays it's more like: "Isn't it funny how a rude thought can change the shape of your cock?"

I didn't make friends easily at school, but as I was no trouble, my teachers allowed me to sink into the background and disappear. School successfully stopped me asking interesting questions and I shut my mouth until I was belched out the other side. Just before this exciting and fearful event, I had a careers interview and was asked about my plans. I had none. Nothing appealed or fitted. I didn't have 'determination to succeed' nor understood what that was supposed to mean. I was intelligent enough to realise that I wasn't intelligent enough to be an astronaut, even if I had the bravery. I mentioned the idea of being a best selling novelist or concert musician but was asked to 'lower my sights a little'. I sensed that some sort of enthusiasm was expected of me, but I couldn't make any sense of it all. Regret, condolences, maybe, but enthusiasm...?

It's easier to talk about the past. In the past, I was someone else, someone I don't really know any more, an old acquaintance that's easier to describe. But who I am now is always in a state of 'becoming' and I can't grasp anything with certainty that might help you picture me. Camus felt the same apparently and he won some great literary prizes, so I must be intelligent like him, eh?

This is my first night alone in this big, anonymous city. I don't know what I'm doing here but I couldn't stand the silence of my room. I had to get out and go down to the student bar. I bought a pint and sat down in a dark corner, surrounded by breasts and bums, laughter, noise, music, the sharp confident clack of pool balls thudding into pockets. It made me want to start my life again, this time with a purpose. These students know what they are doing here. They are starting a future for themselves. I'm here to escape the future and to prove to myself that I'm not thick. I'd like to make friends but I don't want to talk about sexism and racism, don't at this moment give a damn about Northern Ireland or South Africa. I don't much care about the exploited and downtrodden in various parts of the world either at the moment. I know this makes me sound like a bastard, and perhaps I am, but I've got to understand my own existence first. When I try to think and act like a 'good' person, there's a voice in my head that takes the piss and holds up my insincerity like a soiled pair of underpants. Being a good, caring and politically aware person seems like such a pose! It's just a way of sending compliments to yourself.

I downed my beer and bought another. When I was a kid, I'd always close my eyes and wonder about my future. What will I do? What will I be? Is my future wife walking around at this moment, wondering about the same things? Is there a tree growing somewhere in the world that my coffin will be made out of?

A big cheer goes up and the balls on the table are rearranged. I must leave now, before I get too drunk. I've seen a few glances already. They are wondering what sort of swot works in the student bar. It's not an essay; it's my life!

November 18th

It's been more than a month since I've written anything - been too busy reading, having tutorials and recovering from hangovers, but I have to tell you about a friend of mine. I met him in the union bar. He came up to me, all sociable and grinning:

"You're doing philosophy aren't you? Saw you in the library fighting some huge tome," he said. I grinned and told him that I hadn't understood a word of what I was reading and how my essay about 'free will' remained stubbornly unwritten with a deadline approaching.

"Steve," he announced, extending a formal hand, and sat down opposite me clutching a full pint as if it were part of his hand, "Psychology, 'Northerner'."

Here we go again with characterisation! This isn't my strong point, apparently, having received numerous rejection slips from editors of short story magazines. I've tried my hand at writing and never got anywhere with it. Just one of a thousand things that others do so much better than me! But some years ago though, I naively sent a stupid sci-fi story to a stupid sci-fi magazine. One character had green hair, a plastic face, skinny as a rake. The other was fat, bald and partly alien. The editor still said that my characters were all the same! So please bear with me when I say that Steve has a northern accent (not surprising since he's a northerner), a monkey-like grin that gives off both humour and a sort of wisdom; he's extrovert, a bit younger than me, etc. There's a definite suggestion of biceps created by dumbbells and thick black hair that he ties back, making him look like some sort of minor Georgian Royal. Sorry I can't tell you much more, but that's basically it. He hasn't got very thin lips, thinning hair, a squashed face, a huge domed head; he doesn't wear any remarkable clothes (Marks & Spencer shirt- green), doesn't sport a monocle - (that's reserved for a much later and much more unlikely character!) He doesn't carry a stick that he taps emphatically on the floor when making a point, but yes, he wears a small silver ring in his right earlobe for no apparent reason. I'll have to forgive him for that. No-one's perfect. I find all this description and characterisation stuff so boring, but if you want Steve to be like some of the above, go ahead and visualise him in that way, it makes no difference to me.

Steve and I got talking. It was a Friday night and we were really getting the beers in, I can tell you! I asked him what the girls were like in Psychology, pointing out the general dearth of fit females in the Philosophy department. It was then that I noticed the wisdom in the grin. Steve went on to explain that in talking about women, what we were really doing was establishing that we are both heterosexuals and that under no circumstances would we be fondling each other's knobs and bottoms later on in the evening. I'm glad that we got this out into the open! But it was hardly necessary as we were both gazing at the females that dripped steadily into the bar, both apparently devoid of the mating rituals that would bring them to us. We were like two sad baboons at the bottom of the hierarchy, oppressed by the dominant males. Well, that's how I thought of it, anyway. As it happens, Steve reckons himself to be a bit of a ladies man, when it suits him, when the mood takes him. I see no reason to disbelieve him.

We talked for most of the night, but our talking soon staggered towards incoherence and began to take some surreal detours, like a mini-bus full of clowns on a day trip to Hiroshima. (No, I don't know what I mean either!) - The epistemology of breasts, a Marxist analysis of lager, whether B F Skinner was a dickhead or not, and more. Steve gave away a disturbing signal that he was going to work and take Psychology seriously. I think a 'scientific understanding of human behaviour' is ridiculous but I kept my mouth shut. I didn't want to lose a friend so soon.

The beer kept flowing, the girls came and went, the music got louder and I was beginning to feel a bit choked by all the smoke. These variables correlated with us getting more and more pissed! Steve asked me, eventually, why I was staring foolishly at my empty glass of beer.

"I'm looking...at its purpose," I slurred through numbed lips and brain. I could hear Steve's jolly laugh echoing outside the cocoon that started enfolding itself around me. I watched him expertly roll a cigarette - solid, sure of his existence, like my empty glass.

"We've all got one of those," he said, licking and lighting his cigarette.

"I haven't found a purpose yet," I said, as if making a bold confession.

"The 'yet' means you're an optimist," Steve said. His white teeth gleamed through designer stubble. I pondered for a moment.

"You know that old saying - an optimist's glass is half full; a pessimist's glass is half empty, right? Mine's got bugger all in it. Does that mean I'm a nihilist? My ex girlfriend called me a nihilist," I said.

"It means that it's your round," said Steve, deflecting my simile or metaphor or whatever it was. He drained his glass and wiped some froth from his upper lip.

"Then my glass would be full, not empty..." I mused.

"You've got it..."

"But... But..."

The imagery was breaking up like a spaceship speeding through my drunk, burning atmosphere. I back peddled.

"If we're just a load of meat created by genes and instincts, and stuff like that, how *can* we have a purpose? Aren't I just a slave to forces acting upon me? I mean, if everything is *caused*, I can't do anything about it, can I? My life's not my own," I slurred and spluttered. I was thinking about the essay.

Steve doesn't really attach much importance to this 'free will' thing. He thinks that we can be seen as both lumps of matter and imaginative beings in control of our lives. He doesn't think that it's a contradiction to see our behaviour as both free *and* determined. He's got it all sussed, but I'm not convinced. I'm never convinced by anyone who has 'certainty', that's why I can't be a theist or an atheist. I don't believe in believing. I think Steve should write the essay for me; I can't get my head around it. Sometimes it makes sense, sometimes it doesn't - that's why it's interesting I suppose. It's a puzzle I'd like to solve - the nearest to an ambition that I've come to.

"Steve," I mumbled, fumbling about my pockets for some cash, "If I could pull my brains out and put it on the table, would that be everything of what I am? I mean...would that pink, mushy stuff really be 'me'?"

My hands mimed the said delicate operation (which could have been mistaken for the removal of an invisible hat). I placed my brain next to my empty glass. Steve grinned and shrugged his shoulders, flicking ash nonchalantly into a plastic ashtray.

"Ultimately, I suppose so, but brains create minds and minds are what we are. The hardware is useless without the software, isn't it?"

Suddenly the music was turned up again and I had to speak louder.

"But surely you'd have to conclude that a mind, or the software, is just an *illusion* if *ultimately* I'm nothing but a body made up of simple chemicals and water," I said, making gestures that parodied my stuporous attempts to talk like a philosopher. "Isn't the very thing that I think of as me, an illusion?"

"Are you going to get those drinks in?" Steve smiled. I could see in his eyes that he thought I was too drunk for him to explain further. I looked with some concern at my feet below the table.

"I seem to have forgotten how to stand up," I said.

"God! A man could die of thirst here!" he laughed. He had two hands behind his head and one leg crossed over the other - a man at peace with the world. He looked as though he had good, positive things on his mind.

I found my money and piled it up on the table, next to my invisible brain.

"But Steve," I continued relentlessly, "You're the expert on the mind. Why does my brain or my mind, or whatever I am, allow me to think ridiculous thoughts and do ridiculous things? Let me give you a 'for instance'..."

I pushed back my chair and hopped five steps backwards, both hands held in imitation of a rabbit, teeth jutting forward. Heads turned in the smoke, away from private conversations. For a brief naked moment there was shock in the air as normal behaviour was disrupted. Steve slapped the table enthusiastically and I watched his face break up into broken shards of laughter and embarrassment, as if dragged away from rationality by a monster of stupidity.

"Millions of years of evolution and the end result is absurdity," I said, sitting down heavily. "Doesn't that show I've got free will? Doesn't that prove that I'm more than just a physical brain?"

Steve eventually calmed down and the faces turned back to their worlds.

"Humour has a purpose," he spluttered. "It's a part of human nature. You haven't violated any natural laws."

I'm confused, you see! Imitating a rabbit jumping backwards doesn't seem explicable in terms of cause and effect to me. Nor does a mind. I can understand 'determinism' when it comes to birds building a nest or a lion attacking its prey or a chimp fishing out termites with a stick, but no animal ever jumped backwards, making silly gestures and movements. It's just not biologically feasible. Absurdity, it seems to me is stronger than logic. Absurdity laughs at all the laws that we try to dig out of nature. Human life is absurd. I was trying to tell Steve this as I staggered back to my room, but he had a calm and confident look in his eye, and I knew he thought I was wrong.

"Dogs chase their tails don't they?" he said. It seemed deeply significant, like he was warning me not to go round and round in search of what couldn't be caught or found. I'm going to listen to what everybody says and learn from them from now on. Anybody who'll talk to me!

Next Morning

Hangover from hell! No escape; feels no better than life threatening illness, yet inspires no sympathy from anyone. Even bravery is out -"Give it to me straight, doctor. It's a hangover, isn't it?"
I feel so dreadful, suppurating between these twisted sheets, and I've missed the lecture on 'Do Numbers exist?'. I'll have to borrow someone's awful notes. Yet again I groan to myself that I'll never do it again. The 'Day After' - too much lager or nuclear war? - It feels pretty much the same to me. Reality has beaten me up for a few quid and left me for dead. I'm so glad there's a sink in this room. I've pissed and puked in it, marvelling at the body's ability to survive my own poisonings. If alcohol is so dreadful, why don't the taste buds evolve a way of rejecting it? How can we enjoy what does us harm? Strange paradox... Excuse me; time to use the sink again!
  I'm not up to doing anything yet, so I thought I'd better tell you a bit more about Steve. I don't want you to think that he's just a cardboard cut out of a character. I've got to do the poor man justice. I've got to write this diary in a convincing way, as if it were fiction. Did I mention the ponytail? I can't remember. But anyway, he's got a small ponytail and an earring. I wish I could understand why. What does it mean? I've never understood fads and fashions and why everyone wants to express their individuality in exactly the same way. Have they not considered the obvious logical difficulty here? He's also got a sovereign ring on one of his fingers. It's like a gold medal for his hand. You just can't help watching it as he raises his pint to his gob, in what seems like smug celebration.
  Steve's a confident sort of guy all over, but not in a noisy way. He makes me think that he's just quietly plotting how to put the world to rights, waiting for the right moment. He tells me in his 'oh, it was nothing' sort of way that he's had numerous women, and confronted with this, I had to exaggerate my one relationship somewhat. I invented a few one-night stands that were so convincing I almost believed them myself. He told me he was bored up north and that this was the place for Psychology and the classy babes. He gives the impression that he can have what the hell he wants in life. He doesn't seem to suffer any kind of anxiety about living. He doesn't give a thought that his smoking habit might kill him and he's not in the least bit bothered that he's not 'seeing anyone' at the moment, not being

afflicted with the same sort of desperate sex drive as I have, it appears.

I'm hungry now and I'm sure there was a packet of crisps in here, yesterday. I'll write some more a bit later on.

Later

Felt just about well enough to walk it off and get out of this horrible, now deserted place. It was quite chilly outside, but I enjoyed the cold air on my face as I walked slowly towards the only expanse of green within reach – a small oasis in the traffic and concrete, an oasis tarnished with dog shit.

I had to cross that busy main road. The pelican crossing bleeped loudly, the sound like needles in my delicate brain, and for a while the snarl of traffic was held at bay by a mere symbol. I find that amazing! How can the colour red hold back all these cars? What really stops them, eh? Nothing! We only *think* that we can't do otherwise. The rules that constrain us are just on the surface; at any moment they could break down, releasing chaos! That's why I can't go to concerts or plays. I'm too worried that I'm going to shout 'Bollocks!' in a quiet, serious moment, because I know that I *could*. I can just imagine a profound Shakespearean scene... " To be or not to be, that is the....*BOLLOCKS!"* - Then the horrified audience turning their heads towards me. Me, wilting and panicking in disbelief of what I just did! We choose order over chaos, but we're all aware of how near chaos could be. I'm fascinated by the chaos I find inside myself, sometimes. Sometimes my emotions kind of 'explode' and it feels like the world is just about to collapse in on itself. I'm glad I haven't got a gun at such moments. I can feel what it's like to want to run amok and I'm often worried that one day I really will!

Anyway, I reached the park without puking, but I still felt sick. My thoughts jumped about, freedom Vs determinism, sex, women's bodies, my future, the expanding universe, the diminishing grant. I spied a park bench, but a tramp was sitting there already, a fellow human being, 'down on his luck', as they say. I felt this sort of empathy that I've often felt, wanting to understand and share in another's experience. He looked shocked and horrified as I approached him.

"Mind if I join you?" I asked.

"Fuck off!"

- A response not entirely unpredictable, but was it a genuine 'fuck off' or a knee jerk, deterministic response, with no free will behind it? Was he just saying what was expected of him in that role? I looked at the tramp and tried to smile. He must have thought I was mad. Talking to one's fellow men can be a symptom of insanity in our odd culture:

"Sorry to bother you," I said, "but can we talk?"

He looked at me with outrage but seemed to begrudgingly accept that I was just another tramp. I must have smelt fairly similar, as I hadn't washed or combed my hair that morning. I could even sense a distant odour of vomit and didn't know if it was coming from him or me.

"This is my bench," he insisted. I nodded, accepting his authority.

"Got any fags?" he barked hopefully.

"No fags, I'm afraid."

I'll try to describe him.... He was filthy; his face was the texture of leather, his hair matted, not balding, about 38 years old, a Scottish accent, the essence of a 'tramp', a living stereotype, a scarcely believable character. Everything he did and said, was surely what all tramps did and said. Was he a social creation, or had he made a choice? Was he just a victim, an effect of a million causes? Research, you see!

"Do you believe in God?" I heard myself say, knowing that this was precisely what I shouldn't have said. I was prompting his lines, letting him play his role to the full. He stood up, waving a filthy, yellowing finger at me, yelling incoherently. I finally managed to make out a sentence through the Scottish slurring.

"Don't you give me none of that crap!" he barked.

"NO! NO!" I pleaded, "I don't think I do either; but if there's no God, we are alone in the universe with no justification for our existence, no absolutes, no reason to choose between good and evil. It's a frightening thought, isn't it?"

"What the fuck are you going on about? What do you want?" he complained.

I thought for a while, pondering over his challenging but simple question. I gave him my answer, telling him that I longed for 'adventure', some sort of 'connection', some sort of understanding. For some reason, I really wanted to write a book....

"Arsehole! Fuck off and leave me alone!" he interrupted. I looked into his eyes. They were bloodshot and even his corneas seemed dirty, yet I knew there had to be something in there, somewhere. He had a history. He was born and was a baby once. I often think about what people were like when they were young and how different they might have turned out if they had different circumstances.

"And what do *you* want?" I said, turning the question back upon him with the irritating gentleness of a counsellor. I didn't know why I was doing this, winding him up, being deliberately provocative. I just wanted to see the world through his eyes, and not mine, for a change. Every day, I spend hours just wondering what it must be like to be someone else. He was in no mood for discussion, apparently.

"Fags! Beer! That's what it's going to cost you if you want to talk to *me*. That's my fee."

He seemed pleased with himself for a brief moment. He almost smiled. I watched the fleas jump out of his coat as he buttoned it up, preparing to walk away. Ah! A sense of humour, a sense of irony! Here was awareness! I longed to speak nonsense, to get away from serious arguments in lectures and seminars that make no difference to anything.

"That sounds reasonable," I said. Did he detect sarcasm, insincerity? He was in his rights to punch me in the face. I was waiting for it, to confirm my suspicion that he was a robot, just like an estate agent, an accountant, a car mechanic.

"I need to know what it feels like to have no job, no money, no status. I want to prepare for my future," I continued, in mock pleading tones, testing and taunting him further. He glared at me; his lips lifting like a red veil over yellow, untended tombstones. It was a pretty horrible sight.

"Get yourself a job, you stupid prick! Go and get a bed at the shelter; don't sell your arse to queers. Stop wasting my time!" he said, wagging the same yellow finger at me and shuffling off, slowly.

He had taken pity on me! I was very touched! There *was* someone in there, someone who knew a hell of a lot more about real life than I did! He knew where he stood in the world and I envied him. I envied his certainty that no effort, no appearance or respectability was worth a thing. He knew how to face and live with reality as it truly is. Some sort of intuition made me sure that I could learn a lot from him.

I walked back to the park's gates. The whole world and its occupants seemed such a fragile and vulnerable place – the birds in the trees, the ducks on the pond, the lone squirrel chasing from one tree to the next. I felt this 'distance', a sort of separation, like I always have done. The hangover did not help.

I looked down at my muddy, flapping shoelaces and bent down to tie them up. There by my feet was a tiny piece of paper, smudged and wet. I picked it up and saw the childish hand-written words: *'my holiday in Cornwall'*. Again, I wanted to make a 'connection' with its author and share in his or her existence and experience. I visualised the innocence, the childish mind, the childish writing and how the paper got torn and found its way to the park. Was it dropped from a satchel, a satchel holding sandwiches wrapped in tin foil? And that mind becoming older and more refined, changing as society demanded, becoming more responsible, witty, confident, sure of what reality is; no more tender mind.

I've always kept an eye out for stray bits of paper - shopping lists, scribbles and doodles, petrol receipts etc. I once found a scrap of paper near to Christmas that damned well nearly made me blub! It listed the presents for 'mum' and 'dad' and several other relations. I knew it was a young girl who had written it and I could feel kindness coming from the paper. I kept it in my pocket for weeks! These things tell a story and create an emotion and a mystery within me, about people, 'others' out there whom I don't know, existing 'behind my back', oblivious of my life, my consciousness, and me oblivious of theirs. Are their lives and their experiences confusing like mine or are they happily living out their roles, animated like cartoons, doing what is expected, feeling what they are programmed to feel – the 'proud father', the 'defiant son', the 'hard working daughter'? We all play these parts; we all need a script to define ourselves. It's too painful to know that we have free will.

It's this illusion that we're fixed 'things' that I want to look into and include in my essay. Why is a polite, well- spoken, altruistic lorry driver a sociological impossibility? Couldn't an accountant say "All right, me 'ole son?" to an important client in a big-tabled business meeting? If we were aware of our freedom, we wouldn't create these personality prisons, these solid identities of 'tramps', 'psychiatrists', 'builders', 'accountants', 'grocers', 'doctors', we'd just be what we really are, not 'things'. But we *want* everyone to be a 'thing' so that we can predict how they will behave, and we *want* to be a 'thing' ourselves.

I was just feeling nicely absorbed and intellectual when suddenly my brain ceased up, stopped dead in its tracks. Suddenly all these thoughts disappeared like snow flakes in a fire. A beautiful girl was walking through the park, slightly hurrying, shopping bags pulling from both shoulders. Her long fair hair was blowing in the breeze. She clutched her coat around her big bosoms. Something was screaming at me from within.

Next day: 3 o'clock

Three o'clock is a funny time when you're skipping lectures and staring at the ceiling — a no-man's land between hangovers and opening time. Sometimes it feels so foolish 'beating the bishop' — what a sad, solitary pursuit! Powerful, insistent and sometimes less than wholesome desires have crept into my brain, depositing dog shit on the pavement to my enlightenment. That's one for the tutorial. If I have desires that I don't want, are they desires? Are undesirable desires, desires? Must discuss this with Steve!

On reflection, I can't understand what possessed me to annoy that tramp. It was obvious how he was going to react; and I *was* taking the piss! I was turning him into the 'straight man' for my own silly little comedy, creating laughs for myself. I shall try to forget what happened. But the image of the beautiful girl has remained in my mind, burned into my brain like a brand. What evolutionary purpose has this? I'd rather not have desires that cannot be satisfied. But perhaps there's a way around it.

The local paper I often flick through is full of adverts for massage parlours where sex is obviously for sale. Some of them are very close by, and I've been giving the matter quite a lot of thought today. Obviously, I've thought about it before, but things seem to have become kind of 'critical' in that department. I know that I should be meeting lots of people, laughing, boozing, doing crazy, student type things, pretending that life is one big happy party, but the truth is, there are two variables that must be considered here. There is the extremely unlikely chance moment when I might find a soul mate and live happily ever after, and there is the extremely strong desire to have sex right now!

"Oh no!" cries my conditioned morality, "Put it out of your mind! Resist your base animal urges for the sake of your self respect."

That's the 'Superego', the internalised parental disapproval, the helpless schoolboy cringing before authority.

"Come on, let's go. The time is now, we are in charge, you have no resistance!" my genes yell in unison- the unsocialised animal, the selfish Id, screaming in anger.

"My pride, my values, my self respect! They are more important," whimpers my conscience, my middle class reflexes, my unexamined conviction of right and wrong.

"Cultural inventions!" The animal self spits back with venom.

I can feel a conflict between biology and culture in microcosm here. I can hear my genes fighting for dominance. I imagine them to be like the tramp, waving their fingers at me. I've had a lot of fingers waved at me in my life:

"We need to jump ship and colonise new territories," they insist.

"But!.."

"Shut it! Listen to us. We are your only true voice. Do what we command!"

My genes are Sociobiologists you see, arguing that all human motivation is based on sex, an animal need created by the genes so that they can reproduce themselves. I get deafened by their insistent voices and their disapproval at their usual resting place. Here I am, in the prime of my reproductive capability and all my gametes are 'goners'. There's a crisis here that must be resolved. I looked again at the adverts and their tantalising euphemisms and wonder again, 'why not'?

"That's more like it!" I hear in my head and various other locations.

"But if I do this, it means that I'm not free!" I said out loud, "I'm just your slave. I can demonstrate my freedom by resistance…"

"What's the point? Why resist what you want? Come on, there's no'sin'here. Stop being such a prude! What harm is it going to do? " was the reasoned point. I saw the weakness in my position, but kept digging, feeling sure that there had to be a reason why I shouldn't go. After all, for society to work, we must all share some moral absolutes - not killing, not stealing, not… No, the genes had a point. I just couldn't find a genuine moral objection to prostitution, not if the woman was doing it of her own free will.

"I think I might treat myself after all," I said out loud, " but it's really only you that's doing this – not me!"

"We are you…You're just our vehicle. 'We created you, " said my genes, "You are here to serve us! Haven't you read any Richard Dawkins, for

God's sake?"

It's one of those days when I feel like I'm going bonkers! I'm losing my grip on what I thought were absolute standards of behaviour that could never be broken. A terrible awareness of freedom is rising up in me. I really can do what ever I like, can't I? I thought about my pressing and inexplicable need for sex again, turning the argument over and over in my head and agreed that there really is nothing false in hunger, thirst or sexual desire, but everything false in their suppression. My resistance to gratification was masochistic, irrational and a remnant of old religious values.

Such watertight logic sent me off to town to find the massage parlour, trudging through litter-strewn streets and the dimly lit warrens of the underground, map in hand like a lost tourist. Arousal and anticipation were boiling within me as I reached the dingy address and rang the top bell as instructed. Part of me begged for an emergency override, to turn and run, but all systems were go. The genes had their foot on the pedal; there was no turning back. The door opened and I was shown to a 'waiting room' by a woman that must have seen better days, but I won't go into what she looked like. Just use your imagination, will you?

"She won't be long," she said. I sat down, looking at the ashtrays, listening to the sound of the busy main road, feeling the pressure of my trousers against my gene projectile system. I watched the swirl of embarrassment, shame, and disbelief spin around in my head and tried to 'just observe', these things, like a Buddhist. It wasn't too late to run for it, but then she appeared, smiling, attractive, welcoming, and all inner debate dissolved.

"Would you like to come this way?" she said with a smile.

I followed her sheepishly, hardly believing that I would soon be touching that body, that mysterious female essence. Negotiations were polite and business-like. I was soon face down receiving a massage. She was superb to look at, but older than she pretended to be. I'm doubly disadvantaged at this point, being both a sexual and writing novice, but suffice to say, I took my trousers off and accepted the small purple square she handed me as readily as she accepted what I had budgeted for food for the next month or so.

"No kissing on the mouth. No aggressive behaviour. You've got twenty minutes," she said with the smile and poise of an air hostess. She reclined on the bed, as if ready for take off, having just demonstrated all the exits and entrances.

After a bit of embarrassing fumbling around, I found the target and embarked upon a successful mission. It was like a riding a bike and physiological memory started to come back like a paraplegic learning to walk again. 'This is real', said a voice in my head, 'I'm doing it! I'm a human being! I'm doing what I evolved to do!' It was the feeling of not being in control; the feeling of my 'culture' dissolving into my animal nature that exhilarated me. There were no ideas to discuss, no clever theories, just thrusting, nothing else!

To get back to the aircraft analogy then, just as I was getting into the swing of things, I had to return to base, all fuel lost over the sea. I had come in too fast and crash landed, undercarriage still up.

"You've still got eighteen minutes and twelve seconds," she said shortly, looking at her wall clock. There was a note of sympathy in her voice that was more painful than derision. But I was now someone completely different to the person who had walked in the door. Orgasm is like the potion used by Dr. Jeckyll - only in reverse. You take the potion and suddenly the animal becomes the normal citizen, all passion gone, just embarrassment and bewilderment. Which one is the real person?

"It's Okay," I said, gathering up my trousers, "I 'd better be going."

Coins fell out of my trouser pockets and raced for cover under the bed. She smiled like a friendly aunt and told me that I still had my 'thing' on. She pointed to the bin in the corner of the room and the box of tissues on the table. (Tissue adverts always show a contented mother wiping a baby's mouth or a beefy bloke blowing his nose in bed. The major use is never hinted at!)

Genes Vs culture, who can say who won? I got what I wanted and so did she, no problem. But something's still not quite right. There was still something missing from the experience. There was that feeling of separation that spoiled it and a redundant awareness of shame crept back into my mind. I walked away, disappointed, as only a man paying for sex could feel. I should have resisted! I should have had some control over my behaviour and directed it towards more fulfilling projects. And what did my genes just get out of this? Just an *act* that ended with a suicidal crash into a rubber wall. There was no connection, no point, no purpose behind it.

I slept for a couple of hours and missed the evening meal. It would have been stuffed pepper too! Instead, I stared at the blank pieces of paper in front of me, trying to get started on the essay. At least I can think clearer; sex has gone out of my mind for a while. The genes must be in retreat, gathering strength until the next time that they insist on crashing into a rubber wall like a million looneys in a padded cell. Anyway, back to this essay!

Essays are always about what someone else has said, aren't they? What goes on in *my* head is apparently worthless. You're never asked to state your feelings. No-one cares what the writer thinks, only what others think. Why can't I write what *I* think? But what *do* I think? Am I 'free'? It feels like I *could* be. That's why I feel so shit. I know I could find a way to change my life, but to what, I don't know. If I felt that I was just a programmed robot, I wouldn't feel this 'angst' about my life, would I? Things that can't control their behaviour don't have sleepless nights.

It feels like I'm neither my biology nor my culture. It was my genes that paid for sex, not me. It was my cultural brainwashing that objected to it, not 'me'. I'm something else, something between the two - a freedom that's trapped on railway lines that other people have laid down. What is the truth? Does it matter? What is the point of effort or struggle? What is the point of resisting your desires or striving to rise above the gutter? What is success and why is it better than failure? I must find the answer to these questions.

Next Day

I sat in the lotus position observing my experience of shame, degradation and moral uncertainty, and thought I'd postpone the next paid sex session for as long as possible. Despite everything, I can't bear the thought of other people knowing what I'm doing. What if someone found out that I'd visited a prostitute? What if that nice girl opposite me knew? The 'other' is there in my head, their prying, judgmental eyes are inescapable. Hell isn't flames and brimstone, it's *other people*, as Sartre said - their very existence, their very thoughts can disable you. Yet in other cases, people can be heaven too, certainly better than I am! If I went out and got knocked down by a car, a doctor and nurse could help me to survive, but a philosopher or psychologist would be crap at the roadside. I can imagine one leaning over my mangled body:

"You're damaged. Can you tell me how this injury impinges upon your values and priorities? What do you think was the primary causative agent in this life threatening scenario?" Useless bastards! But an ambulance driver would be a much more welcome sight. Trained people, serving others, being altruistic and all that 'good' stuff. I respect that, and I can't imagine why anyone would want to do it. I can't think of any self- centred reasons for working all hours with blood, sick and pus. They have trained to be a 'helping machine' - they work automatically and don't ponder upon the bodies and blood. Somehow, they must be the highest form of human being. I wish I could be sincerely 'good' like they are. Or am I wrong? Are they just on automatic pilot? Are they just a cog in the ever- turning machine? Do they privately think, "I'm not doing this anymore, I'm going to be a folk singer, a painter, an artist. I'm not a robot. I have free will. I want out!" Is everyone pretending that they *are* what they *do*? Sex, music, beer, laughter, that's what I want; isn't that what everyone wants? Why would I want anything else? Why should I be a 'good person' and help others? As I said to my teacher in the careers interview, "Why should I want to *be* something?"

February

Christmas has come and gone. It's funny going home and sleeping in the room you slept in all your life. Dad had managed to re-decorate the room and burn all my old porno mags that I had at the bottom of my drawer. (Well, he *said* he burnt them anyway.) He didn't say much over Christmas. It was almost as if he knew that my pretensions at being a philosopher wouldn't come to anything and eventually, he'd have to bale me out as usual. He was always a good dad- better than most. He never beat me up, never tried to bugger me and never spent his wages on booze instead of food for his sons. I have two brothers. I'll tell you about them...

Wolfgang, (sadly for him, my mother loved Mozart!) had no problems in creating an identity for himself. He had all the tools to hand - a good education, ambition, middle class aspirations, a respectable level of facial hair etc. He knew how to talk and interact with the right sort of people in the right sort of way, gradually absorbing his chosen role more and more. He became a successful businessman, a husband and a father and reached his carefully planned destination – respectability and social acceptance. To top it all, out of the blue he 'found Jesus'. Suddenly, all the impossible things that happened in the Bible were all true - walking on water, child-bearing virgins, feeding thousands of people with a few loaves and fishes, Noah reaching the age of nine hundred and fifty before croaking (- the only wrinkly with nine telegrams from the queen on his mantelpiece.)...It was all Okay with him! Just a few years prior to this defection we'd laughed and joked about it all, but he'd found a new group of friends who had chipped away at his resistance to the impossible. He had made his decision – happiness is more important than the truth. Now that he's discovered that he's going to live forever in eternal bliss, he doesn't laugh much any more! I don't get it!

It felt very discordant giving a bottle of aftershave to someone who thought it fair and just that I, along with the rest of his close relations, were going to burn in hell for all eternity for not believing what he believes. He had, after all, grown a beard again.

My other brother, Michelangelo, (It was those art evening classes!) calls religion 'BLS' - 'Bloody Load of Shit'! He likes football and curry and computers and cars and he can't be bothered with anything cerebral. He's an atheist by default. He's got better things to do than even think about the question. I'm something in the middle, if you know what I mean. I want the truth but don't know if I can handle it. It's odd how we are so different, yet we've had the same background and the same parents. How come we don't all inherit or develop the same minds, eh?

Now, my mother, she is a clever old girl, (except perhaps her ability to name babies). She caught me smoking cannabis when I was 16. Instead of giving me a telling me off she demanded that I roll her a Joint. She smoked one and snapped open a few beers and we had a great evening. I think she wanted to deter me by putting me off by 'mum does it too' - like Bingo or ballroom dancing, but instead she went on day trips to Amsterdam and had a second youth. Dad was not impressed and he blamed me, I think.

I used to write poems in that room –poems and songs and stories, thinking it was only a matter of time before I would be 'discovered'. My ego fell with a crash when I realised that my youth didn't bring swarms of teenage girls to my bed. When I got depressed, it began to dawn on me that my stuff just wasn't good enough and that I wasn't going to be famous. Then I met Anny.... I was 18; she was 20. She chatted me up in an apple-packing factory. We were the only two who showed danger of brain death at the never- ending conversation about football. She introduced me to sex. I was expecting a great torrent of ecstasy; instead it was a fumble and a foolish failure. I felt cheated. But we practised and got it right eventually. By the time I'd mastered it, I was like a small child who'd opened all his presents at Christmas and all excitement was over. How could the fantasy be better than the reality? It didn't make sense! Well, that was the beginning and I've already mentioned the ending. Here's some of the middle:

It was a while before I realised what an utter snob Anny was. The other workers in the factory saw it straight away but my judgement had been clouded by my gratitude that she had disposed of my unwanted virginity. She wanted me to better myself, do some reading, get some qualifications. I remember our first row. I can't remember what sparked it off but I do remember pointing out that she was just 'the pot calling the kettle black', since she too worked in a crappy old factory. She laughed horribly. It sent shudders down my spine! It had a distinctly equine sort of neigh, complete with flaring nostrils and a shaking mane.

"You fool!" she said, "I don't have to do this! I was looking for a 'bit of rough', and to be honest, you weren't really what I had in mind!"

She was a university student, just earning some extra money during the summer break and looking for someone to dominate. I think I reminded her of her superiority. I resolved to get back at her by getting a degree myself one day. Philosophy hadn't yet sprung to mind. I had no idea that my weird feelings about the world and reality had already been written about by really clever people.

"What's the matter? Don't the brainy blokes want to fuck you, then?"

My cheek stung for days after that, but it wasn't long before we were back in bed and began our first 'hate sex' session. She would then turn up at my bed-sit at all hours, nostrils flaring, champing on the bit. In a posh voice she'd whisper into the darkness.

"I want you to fuck me hard! Don't show me any mercy!"

It seemed churlish to say no! She was like a thing possessed at this time, like she was trying to escape something, turn into something -an animal. I wasn't much different. The sex was a battle- ground between two struggling souls. She knew that she wasn't very attractive, as I knew this about myself, and we were both avenging ourselves of the love we couldn't give and the life we couldn't lead. I was soon evicted from that bed-sit. I still fantasise about what happened and long for something similar to occur again but I'm no good at 'playing the game' and chatting women up, as you've probably guessed! I'll show you what I mean. The following ridiculous conversation occurred between me and an absolutely stunning female who was unlucky enough to find herself dancing with me at a student party earlier in the term. I stared at her for a few mind- numbing seconds before speaking. I knew it would be absurd:

"What are you studying then?"

How I hated myself for saying this stupid line! Her smile killed me; she'd heard it a thousand times. Her lips were all stretched across tiny, pretty teeth and these little dimples appeared in her cheeks. It was terrible! She had a small silver replica of a Roman instrument of torture hanging round her perfect throat but I barely noticed it. Fireworks were going off in my veins, but the mask was well glued to my mug.

"Geography and speech therapy. I'll be able to give my patients good directions," she said.

I laughed, loving her wit. I wanted to marry her, there and then, impregnate her, protect her and my offspring from predators! In an instant, I knew that she was 'right' for me, (just as every day at approximately thirty minute intervals, I see a woman that's just 'right' for me). It was there in her skeletal structure, the shape of her hips and breasts, the health of her skin and hair. And the smile! It was like a symphony, a meadow full of wild flowers. All my yearnings stood before me, inches from resolution! My genes were at it again, full of orders and demands - the 'Id' screaming again like yobbos in a football stadium, its beastly little finger in my back - "Fuck her! Fuck her!" I tried to shake the little demon off and contemplate her spiritually. This angel was dancing with 'ego', whilst superego wasn't feeling too super at this point - pretty much redundant. Old 'super' only emerges when I pay for it, so it seems. It's just that Id bastard and me now. Then suddenly I was talking about where she had come from.

"Norwich? Oh yes, I know Norwich. It's got lots of roads and...beaches, I think. It's nice there...Yes, I passed through it once. There were road works at the time.... There are a lot of roads there, I think. Is that right? " I said. I found myself thinking about Norwich and all the people there that I don't know.

"Roads?" she says with a puzzled face. I've blown it! She wants to wait for her moment and then get away without appearing to escape. I understand what she's doing and wish I could tell her. If I could be authentic to myself, I'd just take her in my arms and make mad passionate love to her, then run through the streets of Norwich as people leant out of their windows, shouting greetings, good wishes and congratulations, instead I'm talking nonsense about roads. A dam that holds back tidal waves isn't interesting. It's just a wall; it's just resistance; it's just a pile of boring old bricks, but what it holds back is a deluge that could engulf everything! I watched her, eventually leaving the hall with an ear-ringed twat.

People are hell!-especially women- women who stir my genes and thwart my dreams. Don't they realise that they *are* a man's self esteem? They are the justification of a man's existence. If attractive women don't want you, you might as well be dead! Prostitutes are for losers...

I felt empty that night. Something felt way out of reach; something pulling at the plug letting everything in my head swirl down the drain. I'm searching for something to make me whole, make me real, to justify my life. It's something to do with women, sex, love, knowledge, truth. That night, the void was too big to close, and even Id lost his motivation and had to drown his sorrows.

Next Morning

I've just read over yesterday's entry and imagined some complete stranger reading this diary. Would he or she give a toss for my 'inner life'? Would he or she be thinking: 'This writing is second rate!'? What if my difficulty in creating believable characters is merely a reflection of real life? Real life characters are wooden, stereotyped and unbelievable too. Real life too is a plotless ramble. We are all false; we're all just writing our own unimportant little stories for our over-inflated little egos. It's just that some people do it better than others. I've got to stay with it! It's my one life and it's all I've got. And most of it isn't even true! Please keep reading. It gets better. I promise. I go completely bonkers!

I skipped another lecture and decided to stare into my mirror, determined to find the truth about myself, to get behind myself, to see what I am:

"Mirror, Mirror on the wall
Am I so ugly that I can't 'pull'?"

Well, I did it before with the crazy woman; surely I can do it again! She wasn't really that crazy to be honest, not at first. Let me tell you a bit more about what happened between us. It won't take long. You see, before we started to hate each other, we pretended to be 'in love'. We hired the props, read the script and we were dedicated to a believable performance. We had candle-lit meals, cards and presents and at first our love- making was profound. But, as time went by, our performances became less than polished. The "I love you" line was edited out of the script. On the odd occasions when it was prompted, the words were coughed out quite quickly like food stuck in the throat. We started to create arguments out of nothing and it took me a while to realise why. We were building up a steam of hostility in order to make the eventual break. We couldn't just part, we had to hate each other first so that the break would be easier. The drama had to have a suitable 'tragic' ending; it couldn't just 'stop'. But then that new dimension emerged from this pretence - those 'hate sex' sessions I mentioned. We both enjoyed this drama and could have gone on like this for years, but even hatred burns itself out in the end to leave the charred remains of indifference. (There's nothing passionate about indifference.) We parted, but my indifference soon turned into the compost of loneliness and I chanced a letter to her:

"Anny, if I ever meant anything to you please write back. I'm feeling really lost, like I don't understand anything. You were my friend. How can we throw that away? What else is there in the world worth having?"

She didn't write back. She turned away from an imploring hand asking for help, whilst the other clutched, bloodily at the rocks that chipped away, sliding in fragments to the abyss below. I was asking for friendship but not even that was left. All the words we said to each other. They meant absolutely nothing, but I think I always knew that. I hated her for having the strength to walk away from an illusion.

The mirror stared back at me. The face just looks the same as it always has. I see no significance to it, can't see it as handsome or ugly; I just presume that it's not film star material. Acne scars sit on my face like physiological graffiti, rude statements put there to offend others. I squeeze a spot, but it resists attack and throws out pain like the spines of a hedgehog. At least I'm not going bald! A mate of mine is years younger than me and he's almost bald! He used to be a wow with the girls with his long rock 'n' roll hair but now he's behind a desk in the civil service as bald as the prophet Elisha.

There are whole swathes of no-go areas on my face where stubble refuses to appear; yet there's enough on my chin and upper lip to justify the morning scrape. It's like a lawn mower bumping over mole- hills and there are always bits that seem to escape the blades. I've always found it odd, walking around with my face exposed to the world. It enters other people's eyes, gets converted to electrical impulses and ends up in their heads where I have no control over their judgements. They've got me then, and they can do what they will with me, heap all manner of insults and derision upon me and I'll never know about it! That has always made me feel uncomfortable.

I push this face deeper into the mirror and watch it disappear, blurring into a hideous mask, just flesh and bone arranged into this shape and colour. What holds me all together? How does my body stay in one piece? How do I go on creating this sense of self? It's all so weird and frightening. Why am I here? What do I believe in? What can justify my life? Shall I try to 'be' something or shall I just drift wherever the wind blows?

5.30

Things are awful, really bloody awful. I feel sick, nauseous, disgusting and I'm not talking just beer and curry. I had to get out of the library and go somewhere away from books. It was like a small voice in my head – my genes again perhaps, telling me that I was deluding myself by just reading and reading. I slammed shut the book I was reading really loudly, making people all around me raise their eyes in my direction.

"What is the point?" I declared dramatically to the library with a great dismissive gesture and stormed out before anyone had thought of laughter as a defence. I felt like I was really slipping and going off my trolley. I made my way to the student Refectory and asked for a coffee. It came in a polystyrene cup. I sat down with it shortly and stared at the traffic outside, trying not to hear surrounding conversation. Then I was seized by it; a terrible need to puke and faint. A doctor would call it a 'panic attack', but such a diagnosis leaves out everything that's important. My GP would give me some drugs to take "three times a day with meals". He wouldn't say: "I think this is a case of existential angst; there's a lot of it about at this time of year, break down of traditional meaning structures, you see. I'll give you a prescription for a belief system. We'll start you off with something supernatural and if that doesn't work, we'll try something a little more secular – 'Nationalism' can be effective in some cases..."

I've tried such prescriptions already, but they don't work for me. I can't be anything. All I know is what I'm not. I'm *not* a Marxist, *not* a Monarchist, *not* a humanist, I'm a NOT; I'm defined by what I don't believe in. I don't belong to any 'club'. I'm baffled when someone says he's 'proud to be Welsh', or 'proud to be black'. How can people be proud of their accent or their melanin? What are they talking about? Someone else's history or someone else's genes say nothing about what *you* are! You can't fill the hole in your head with an honorary heritage! You get people saying things like *'we don't know whether we are English or Indian.'* Why must they have an identity when all identities are inventions? People say 'I'm proud of my religion' too. What does that mean? How can you be proud of what is supposed to be the 'truth'? They're not talking about truth; they're talking about identity! They're proud that they're something that others are not! The truth is, nothing can *really* define you so you have to find something false that will give you an identity. As Sartre said, *Existence comes before essence.* We have to invent who we are but an 'essence' always eludes us. So if I decide that I'm an 'existentialist', I'm being fake and pretentious, a pseudo- intellectual trying to rise above Joe average. I'm trying to define who I am. I cannot be an existentialist because I am an existentialist! I have to live with *no* identity because I know the truth and I'll dance with the truth like she were a woman. With outstretched arms, I'll embrace the wraith of loneliness and breathe her fragrance of indifference (Poetic, eh?).

I have this perverse desire for the 'real', you see - for *reality*. A bunch of plastic flowers looks lovely and lasts forever. Real flowers don't last, can't be distinguished from fakes- the better option, yet I choose the vulnerable, the real. Funerals are 'real' and the religious ritual reveals their true nature. At funerals, crap transubstantiates into kindness and you can almost forgive the lies. The truth no longer seems important, only feelings matter at such times. That's why funerals are uplifting. It's not that I'm a 'sicko'!

(I remember a friend's funeral I went to. He was a jazz musician and we always got on really well. He was a hell of an enormous bloke, I can tell you! He must have weighed as much as a shire horse. He was massive! We went for a drink many a Tuesday night and what made me laugh inside was that he always had a rum and *diet* coke. He would then devour a huge curry at his favourite 'Indian'.

I once said to him, "Do you believe in life after death?" and he gave me that 'Who cares?' shake of his head that made his chins wobble.

"That's an interesting question for about five minutes," he said, " Then I can't be bothered to think about it."

He died suddenly of a massive heart attack. It was one of his fears. He told me in the pub. He once went to a doctor and asked for some pills because he was worried that there might be something wrong with his heart. The doctor told him to go away and lose some weight, but he never did. Food was all he had. He didn't drink; he couldn't have sex, so he ate.

It took more than six men to carry his coffin. I saw a couple of them exchange a grin of anticipation before they picked it up. They didn't know I could see them. I wanted to laugh too. That sounds terrible, but I could feel his 'spirit', taking the mick, enjoying the strain he was putting on those shoulders.) –Sorry about that long digression….

None of these musings took my mind off this nausea. The coffee tasted disgusting and conversations assaulted my ears. Two ear-ringed confident intellectuals were jabbering on about 'ideology' and 'Hegemony' and 'the working class'. They were playing a game of "who's the cleverest? Who's the most articulate?" I clutched my stomach. Sweat began to drip from my forehead. I wanted to tear out those silly insignificant earrings, but couldn't open my mouth. I was seized by a terror that vomit was about to spurt forth, rupturing the thin social fabric that we all drape around ourselves. Vomit, farts, screams all give us away and destroy the illusion of order. That's why we are so afraid of them and make jokes about them.

Sinking deeper into this nausea, the smoke seemed to solidify into glass that surrounded itself around me, cut off from my fellow human beings, no feeling or connection, just isolation, bewilderment and contempt. I was watching and listening to robots, programmed to appear 'deep', intellectual, purposeful, responsible, qualities that enhance the sense of self. Phoney, phoney, phoney! These are not like the ambulance drivers. Their 'thingness' is for themselves, not for others. Hostility, compassion, sexual frustration, indigestion, spinning upwards like the debris in a hurricane. I wish I could see them at the age of 3 or 4, pushing a toy bus along the carpet, just doing what a child does without that inner 'mirror' that tells you how clever you are, just being what you are, without knowledge.

I wonder what I'm doing here, in this moment, in this time. I look at maps, road maps. I open an Atlas and turn to a page at random and look at a town name, imagining what life is like there, the tragedies, comedies and controversies. I wonder if there's a woman there that I could fall in love with or have an amazing bonk with. What's happening in Uppingham or Rawtenstall, Cliburn, Kilwinning or Sandford? How many beauties are there in Yatton, and what are their names? What party is being prepared in Coombe Bisset? How many people have tried to write a novel in Norwich? What pain, what glories exist there?

Sometimes, I get into a train and go somewhere I've never been before, look around and go back again with this incomprehensible feeling, having never met all those 'others' I'll never, ever know. But these buggers have 'fixed' themselves; they've decided what they are and how they'll see the world, decided on the course of their future. Yet, they've at least made a commitment. They've 'become', they have a 'direction', they've invented themselves and are convinced by it. But I can't choose yet, can't find anything to believe in, can't find any convincing story to believe about myself or anything else. Nothing can give me an identity. Worthwhile projects exist for others, but not for me.

Values are flimsy when you hold them up to the light – transparent and easily destroyed, like butterfly wings. Was that why I fucked the prostitute, to give away these values that have become a part of me like invading viruses? Was I merely ridding myself of a morality that had no real existence? Was I in control, not my genes? Was it an act of free will after all? I can interpret my motives in anyway I choose, but if I don't believe my own lies, I can't be authentic. Authenticity can only happen when my values are totally mine and not something I've accepted from others.

...I do realise that a lot of that should have been edited out, but I'm leaving it in out of defiance! Dissonance in music or writing is not necessarily wrong; it has a distinct emotional effect! Plenty more where that came from! Having cleared that up, let's get on with the story...

I had to leave my disgusting coffee on the table and get some fresh air. I stumbled out, looking for somewhere to be discretely sick, but the air seemed to abate it, and I found myself walking in the direction of the park again. This time, I took a detour and stopped off at an Off License to get a couple of cans of strong lager. I eventually found 'Jock' (that's what he calls himself). He didn't look pleased to see me, but when he saw the beer cans, he seemed to perk up. He accepted one without thanks and snapped it open, before taking a huge swig.

"What the fuck do you want now?" he asked.

"I've got to write an essay about Free will," I said, "And I want to talk to people who really know freedom, people that can do what they like and not care what others think of them," I said.

"Oh yeah!" said Jock, taking another swig. "You make having fuck all sound exciting. Well it ain't! Before I got like this I thought life was something you had to work at and get right, but it was all shite; I can't be arsed anymore."

"But that's my point," I said, " You can't be arsed. But I still can't rid myself of the idea that success is better than failure. Can you help me shake this off? Can you tell me what the secret is? "

Jock lifted a buttock and farted resoundingly. I wondered if there was a special message in this but could not think of what he might have meant. I opened a can for myself, whilst thinking about his attitude. He didn't care about anything. Without even thinking about it, he knew that going up or going down the ladder was essentially the same daft act. He'd kicked the ladder aside. He was as good as any Buddhist teacher. I wondered at first if his 'trampness' was just a false identity that he'd created for himself - a secure stereotype. But now I think he's just 'real' - a man without identity. He seemed to really 'know' something that others didn't. I wanted to learn how he achieved this enlightenment. Is this madness or the truth or both?

"Have you got fags this time?" he said, impatiently.

"I'll bring fags next time, I promise."

Jock looked at me with bleary carefulness. I could see the dust in his wrinkles as he screwed up his eyes. Broken, irregular teeth peeped through a grimace.

"I don't like poofs or religious idiots," he said.

"Don't worry, I'm neither of those," I said.

"You're not a Man United fan are you?"

I shook my head diplomatically, not wanting to offend him by stating that I had no strong football convictions. I'm always careful not to offend in such matters. We live in a multi-team culture now and I understand that all of them should be respected as merely different routes to the same essence of football.

"So what are you then? What the fuck do you want?" said Jock, exasperated.

"I'm fed up with people who've got a purpose. I think it's better to be honestly nothing than dishonestly something, but I can't manage either..."

"I don't know what you're talking about and I don't care. You're talking shit, mate."

"Probably, yes. But what isn't shit? That's what I want to know."

"Nothing," said Jock, finishing his can and placing it under the bench. "There's nothing that isn't shit. You just have to live from day to day. That's it. Okay? Are you happy now?"

"Your excremental analogy isn't very different from Eastern ideas of 'emptiness'..."

"Shut up, arsehole, I'm a busy man. I've got to get going..." That irony again! It was a yellow finger pointing to the moon. Jock stood up and abruptly steadied himself.

"What is real, Jock?" I said, trying to keep him from leaving, "I've got to know." He looked at me, frowning and scratching his head.

Jock looked at me in disgust and confusion and walked off, muttering that I was a 'fucking nutter' and that next time I should bring some fags. I finished my can and started laughing joyfully. The nausea dissolved like ice cream in a Jacuzzi. It was like a brief flash of revelation, my life seemed ridiculous, but for a moment ridiculous without the anxiety – comical. The searching, the questioning, all seemed to be ridiculous when 'everything is shit'. Jock was a wise man and he had given me insight.

Friday 3pm

I've always stared out of windows and watched time pass by. I've watched it grow dark and seen the first lights come on in the street; watched people come home, open their front doors and disappear into their invisible worlds. I've wondered if people still exist when I can't see them. To me, a person only exists when they are in my mind; they are just mental impressions. Dead people are also alive, or maybe more alive than the living people that I'll never meet. I can forget living people more easily than dead people, unless I know them well. So many come and go, appear and disappear in my mind. They need me to keep them alive.

I sometimes resurrect Anny and go through our fucks and our fights, keeping her alive. She screamed at me, saying I was a useless 'no-hoper' and that I'd never do anything with my life. Her 'doing something' amounted to 'having things' and the embracing of hard work as life's ultimate purpose. I think she wanted me to accept these values more than her as this is apparently more appropriate to the penis- endowed variety of humans. What is she doing now, four years down the line? Does she ever think of me? Perhaps Descartes got it wrong. Perhaps it should be "*I think, therefore you are, and you think, therefore I am.*" That makes more sense to me. It's why some people just have to have loads of friends. The more people that know you, the more you 'are'. Sometimes I think it's better not to think: "I don't think, therefore I am free..." This is philosophy turned on its head. This is what Zen and eastern philosophy is all about. Either this is what I've been looking for or else it's a cop-out and it suits my ego to believe that all knowledge is pointless and that there's no self because it would be a welcome relief to know that this self that I'm stuck with doesn't really exist. But to hate yourself is a cop-out too. There's no escape, you've got to go through with it, whatever that is. No other way is authentic or acceptable. I'd like to put all this into my essay.

So are we free? Some people are, some aren't. We're free when nothing ties us down; when we're not taken in by religion, our culture, our folklore, our tradition, our background, peer pressure, expectation, our own psychology. I reject the values that make me a robot, but if I embrace totally new ones that liberate me, I just become a different robot with a different programming. I can't escape being a stereotype. I can't escape choosing to be something when I don't want to choose. I want to just be what I am. I want to be free to be what I am but I can't find the *am* for me to *be*...

Are we free? If we're free, where does it come from when everything else has a cause? Something that exists without a cause is religious mumbo-jumbo. If we are not free, then how can I be responsible for anything? I might as well rape and kill and I wouldn't be to blame, but I know I *am* responsible for what I do. I *can* choose.

Do you know what Dostoevsky said? He reckoned that if we managed to work it all out rationally and know how to live without any trouble or need, we'd rebel! We'd deliberately do terrible things just to prove that we can't be tied down! He was right, I reckon!

I don't know if I'm free or not. I feel free but I also feel like a puppet on a string. Those genes of mine swing my legs in unnatural arcs towards massage parlours. I go where the strings pull me. What is this punishing drive that never ceases? I can never be free from it. I don't want loads of babies! Why do my genes insist that I do? Existence is hard to get your head around. Writing an essay doesn't seem important, going to university doesn't seem important, but I've got to keep a few strings up there to move me. If I cut them all for authenticity, would I fall in a heap; a pile of wood that would never get up again? I'm like Pinocchio, made of wood, but capable of being real, but 'wood' is the norm, wood is the way I'm used to and seen in others. And I want to be real, whatever that can mean.

I was thinking all these deep and daft thoughts as I made my reluctant way to see Professor Hines, my tutor. I had to go and see him, probably something about the essay that hadn't been done. I made my way through the corridors and outside towards the cosy older buildings that housed the department of philosophy. They had creaky doors and creaky staircases with smooth, black banisters. I felt like a school- boy going to see the head master. I knocked on the door, just below the wooden plaque that confirmed his prestigious existence. After a short while, he opened it himself, as if it were his home. He didn't recognise me or know why I was standing there.

"Yes?" he said. He had a pen in his hand and there was a funny sort of whiff about him. He seemed a bit bothered. I had probably disturbed him in some deep philosophical problem. He had obviously forgotten about our appointment.

Professor Hines (if you think it's important) is about 60 years old. His hair is wispy and grey. His forearms and fingers are skeletal – delicate brown branches that sprout from his white rolled up sleeves. He wears a harmless badge of eccentricity – a small bow tie with blue dots on it. It has humour in it, perhaps a touch of irony. I'm not sure. He dresses as if to say, "I'm old and I don't care". The books he has written himself are in untidy, dusty rows on the top of his bookcase, as if they didn't matter too much to him. Was he egoless, or was he sending out an image to others, dressing down to draw attention to himself? I had no idea. I stood for a few seconds, but nothing clicked.

"You wanted to see me. There was a note in my pigeon hole."

"Oh… Oh yes! Do come in. And you are?"

"That's a question I'm trying to find an answer to," I said with a grin.

"Sorry?"

For such a brilliant mind, he was a bit thick really. No sense of humour.

"I thought you were asking an existential question," I persisted, feeling a little foolish.

He looked at me as if I was totally mad. He was in another world to me and not even humour could bridge the gulf. Not even philosophy! I stopped trying to be funny and gave him my name. He asked me to sit down. There was a big pile of papers on the chair that he had not noticed. I remained standing. Confusion started to rise up like small bubbles until he noticed why I wasn't sitting down. He mumbled an apology and moved the papers into another precarious pile on his desk.

"I ...er... I don't seem to recognise the face," he said, pulling a wad of more papers from a filing cabinet. I thought it unwise to offer a possible reason why that might be the case, so I just said, "Oh."

"Ah yes!" said Hines, eventually. "Have you, erm... Have you found somewhere to live yet?"

"I've been in the Hall of residence since the first term."

"Good. Excellent. Excellent. And er, how are you finding the course?"

The awkward conversation stumbled along for ten minutes or so. Eventually, we brought up the question of the unwritten essay and when I was going to present my seminar. The seminar was something that I had not wanted to think about. I'd been to a few and watched the show. They were nothing to do with learning anything, they were just auditions, people showing how good they can talk. I was hoping to slip into the shadows and be forgotten. I could tell he didn't really like me. He thought I was a time-waster, a nerd studying philosophy for a free ride. He had eyes, like Anny, that accused.

"I'm trying to write the essay but I keep getting confused about it all. Sometimes I'm free, sometimes I'm controlled by something. Sometimes I'm responsible, sometimes I can't help it..."

"Attending the lectures and seminars can sometimes help to clear the confusion in philosophical issues," he said.

I allowed his knife to sink in. It wasn't too close to the heart, but it was aimed to puncture a lung or graze a rib.

"I wanted to find the answer in my own experience. I didn't want to recycle other people's ideas on it..."

Hines smiled cynically. He wasn't really bothered and yes, he was a frosty old git! I could tell he had something on his mind that he wanted to get back to. He had a job to do. His search for truth and meaning was now an academic, administrative routine. He was like the vicar taking tea with the laity, swapping existential questions for the opening of fetes.

"The seminar?" he said, pencil twitching impatiently between his fingers.

"I'm working on a few ideas..."

"I'm putting you down for three weeks time. I hope that's all right."

"Fine!" I said to the executioner, squeezing my death into my filofax. A sense of dread crept upon me.

"And the essay in fairly soon?" said Hines.

I nodded. Was he enjoying this? It was hard to tell. Nobody can reveal his real life and experience. We are all inventing ourselves and bouncing off other people to hear our own echoes. We are all trapped in this 'self' prison. This silly old sod had a bit of power to use on me. It was probably the only pleasure he could get. He was delaying the pleasure of kicking me out so it would be all the more enjoyable later. Hines put some papers back into the drawer and tried to make some sort of order of his desk. He looked slightly stressed. Perhaps if I helped him, I thought, he might give me an extension on the essay.

"Do you want a hand with all this?" I said, standing up and reaching for a pile of papers that were scattered loosely on his desk. He protested as I started to gather them up and quickly snatched the porno magazine from my hand that the papers had been covering. I smiled, delighting in my discovery that he too was a normal human being, but he took the smile to be a threat. I could see the paranoia churning away there, envisioning blackmail and scandal.

"Hey, don't worry! " I said, but I couldn't help the chuckle that tickled my insides. This was comedy, reality punching through the facade and catching us unawares.

"Your essay has to be in tomorrow! " he said.

"Okay. Okay...but please, don't worry about..." But then I started laughing again. He practically kicked me out and I chuckled uncontrollably back down the stairs. It was an inspiring moment.

With renewed motivation, I went back and wrote the essay with all the authenticity I could muster and sat back with a feeling of satisfaction. I put it in Hines' pigeonhole and went to find Steve. I found him in the library, seemingly taking life too seriously, reading some huge book on social psychology. Great big, thick books ooze self importance, almost challenging the reader - "Come on, you're never going to get to the end of this are you! I might as well make the last few hundred pages a load of crap!" But Steve was studying it intently.

"Let's go for a drink," I whispered, " I've got some scandal."

He gave a fair impression of being in conflict between work and a drink but made a snap decision.

"OK!" The book snapped shut and several people looked up, indignantly.

"Sorry," we whispered simultaneously.

Steve took the book out, carrying it under his arm like a bloody tombstone – intellectual diving ballast! Shows everyone that you're capable of going very deep indeed. I partially understood him, partially connected with him. But there was something 'between us', some sort of 'other world ness', like with Hines, like with Anny, like with every other human being I've ever met- a secret, incomprehensible *self* lingering there in the midst of frankness and honesty. This didn't stop us from getting good and drunk and Steve firing up some potent 'Skunk', guaranteed to cause amnesia and stupidity within 10 minutes. Steve passed the Joint across the table. We laughed about Hines and about our futures. Steve seemed to have a better idea about his than I did, though. He had a plan. Although he liked a drink and a spliff, he wanted to take Psychology seriously and get somewhere with it, but at the moment he was also happy just to enjoy himself.

"And when you get your degree, what are you going to do with it?" he asked.

I took a huge toke and glanced appreciatively at the smouldering end. The red glow was like a wink or a grin. It seemed to tickle me from somewhere deep inside.

"Like my penis," I remember saying mysteriously, "I expect I'll look at it with admiration but feel regret for its lack of real purpose, you know?"

Steve seemed to find this quip funnier than I had expected, no doubt influenced by the 'Skunk'. He fell over backwards, laughing, spilling his beer all over himself, the table and the floor. I put down the Joint, and giggling stupidly, tried to help him to his feet. Steve tried to steady himself by grasping the end of the table. He managed to pull the whole thing over, sending the ashtray and its brimming contents bouncing across the floor. Steve was on his back again, flat out, amongst the ash and a beer ocean. It was the funniest thing in the world! Funnier all the more by the very fact that it just wasn't funny at all! We saw through the posturing of other students who were laughing too. They were laughing at a 'Punch and Judy' show, but our laughter was at life itself. The more they laughed, the more we laughed at them laughing. We were right in there – the absurd, two wine corks bouncing about on the waves, laughing at our existence. Eventually, we were forcibly ejected from the union bar. I remember the hands on my shoulder and the sensation of moving without using my limbs.

"This is 'bad faith', my friend," I said to a hairy knuckle. "You're not your role, you know. You have internalised a false self image that..."

* * *

I've never watched traffic from such a perspective before. It was very interesting, wheels turning; the smell of dog shit. Steve helped me up and we checked for injuries.

"This is like war, isn't it?" I said. "Two soldiers going into battle. It's a real adventure!"

"It's certainly fascinating," said Steve, like Mr sodding Spock. He was still being the academic whilst stoned and pissed. When I'm pissed like this, I feel free; I've no past, no future, not even a present and marijuana helps obliterate the past. I patted Steve's shoulder, half holding myself up.

"Got any more spliffs?" I asked him. Steve nodded, his usual monkey grin seemed more spread about on his face and his eyes swivelled unsteadily.

"Let's go to the park. I want you to meet my friend," I said.

"I think I just want to go to bed," said Steve.

"No, come on!" I insisted.

I pushed Steve forward towards the road with its odd rushing noise and its even stranger blinding moving lights. We were like Space explorers on a new and alien planet. I pressed the button at the crossing and watched the word 'WAIT' light up the darkness.

"For what?" I laughed. Steve wasn't with it. I pointed at the sign and tried to focus on him; "Wait for what?"

"Er, Christmas?" Steve offered.

The lights went green and the 'Wait' sign disappeared. I wanted to write a poem about the 'wait' sign of life disappearing, allowing us all to cross our busy main roads of thinking. Cool!

"Who's this friend of yours?" said Steve, his earring glinting in a headlamp.

"Jock. He lives in this park. He's a social reject, like us."

"You speak for yourself," said Steve, and he meant it.

A fox screamed like a terrified girl being raped. A figure wrapped in newspaper stirred on a bench in the distance, barely visible in the darkness.

"Jock!" I called out. "I've got some fags!"

A faint groan came out of the darkness and then some muffled swearing. Steve and I managed to get over a wall and into the park that had been officially closed for hours.

"Why can't you leave me alone?" said Jock, mournfully. As we approached, he sat upright and pointed the finger.

"You're pissed!" he said with more envy than indignation, "Didn't you bring me any beers?"

"You wanted fags!"

"Beer *and* fags!"

"We've got fags," I said. Steve took out the Joints and we all lit one.

"This is dope, isn't it?" said Jock with what seemed like irritation, but he carried on smoking it with enthusiasm. I introduced him to Steve. They both made a couple of grunts of acknowledgement.

"Now will you talk?" I asked, and he did. He was born in Glasgow. He bunked off school, he got a job repairing cars, got married but was divorced soon after he started hitting her and drinking too much. He got into trouble with the police for thieving and fighting, eventually getting 'banged up' for a couple of years. He lost his job and home and wife and couldn't get anything other than a bit of labouring here and there. He drifted down to London, but couldn't get settled and ended up sleeping rough. I didn't want to offend Jock, but I was disappointed.

"That's just the stereotype, Jock," I said. "That's just a definition of a tramp, a cliché. You've just read the script. You've conformed to what a tramp is supposed to be. You've let me down!"

The Joints glowed in the darkness, lighting up three vacant expressions.

"You're both a couple of wankers," he said.

Why did I want to bridge this gap between two conscious minds? Perhaps there really is nothing beyond the roles we play. When we remove the costumes, we disappear. We are all dead bodies, zombies, puppets, acting. The act is the reality. I don't know if this is right or not. I don't know anything. I'm Socrates today. The more I learn, the more I learn that I don't know...

"Did you know that gorillas have very small balls?" said Steve, suddenly.

Jock cackled and snorted, now cheerful. Just as you would expect a drunk, stereotyped tramp high on dope to be. He'd heard the word 'balls' and laughed – a conditioned response. I laughed too, laughing at the tramp that laughed for all the wrong reasons.

"Steve," I said, "If life were a work of fiction, which it probably is, you've just made a terrible gaff."

Steve's eyes rolled in my direction, swivelling with incomprehension. I continued my point.

"Well, you see..." I said, " Up 'til now, the reader would be thinking that I'm the unstable one, but you've just demonstrated a similar character trait to me. You've said something out of context and irrelevant."

Steve took another toke, lost in thought for a while.

"Not at all..." he said eventually. "I was making a real scientific point. I read it today. It's a *fact* that gorillas have small balls."

Jock laughed. The sound of his laugh was shocking – out of context. There was misunderstanding in it. He cut himself off from the joke. He was laughing at the empty sky, laughing at nothing.

"And why's that, Steve?" I said, shaping my character to match Steve's. The interaction was flowing beautifully down a river of nonsense, without resistance, without competing for status.

"It's because they have no competition for females, you see. They don't have to create much sperm. If you've only got six screws to screw in, you don't need a huge great toolbox, do you?"

Jock didn't laugh. I noted that he couldn't think symbolically. His sense of humour had to be dirty words, 'balls', 'fuck', 'shit' etc. He was like a drunk at a tennis match, knowing that something was going on but not sure of the rules. It was going to be difficult to be like him, if that really was my ambition.

"But chimps have *big* bollocks," said Steve.

Jock laughed, cackled, enjoying himself. A feeling of superiority arose within my drunken brain, but another part of me knew that I was as stupid as Jock if I imagined that I was in any way superior to him. Everyone you meet is just a reflection of some aspect of yourself, or something. Isn't that right?

"And why's that, Steve?" I enquired.

"Because they have to produce more sperm, you see? Their sperms have to compete with other sperm..."

"Chimps fuck a lot then?" Jock deduced.

"Erm, yes, I think so..."

"That's interesting," said Jock. I was stumped! If he meant it, the stereotype was broken. If he was being ironic, again the stereotype was broken. Tramps don't say that sort of thing! Jock was being 'real', not just a thin, cardboard character. My faith in him had returned. If only I could get him to really speak his mind! There had to be a way...

"So, if I've got big balls, I fuck a lot," said Jock, exhaling a cloud of smoke.

Steve's head swung gently in the time of his struggling thinking.

"Erm, no. If you've got small balls, you fuck a lot, because you're the only one that's doing the fucking. I think so, anyway."

"So big balls mean I fuck lots of different women then, does it?"

"Theory and practice can sometimes be at variance," I said, pissing myself.

"What's that?" said Jock.

The conversation was slipping away and becoming more and more pointless with every breath.

I floated on a cloud of cannabis, at one with the absurd.

"Someone's just grafted their ideas onto reality, " I said, my voice echoing out into the star pierced canvas of the night. " Reality escapes all this clever theorising and..."

"Crap!" said Steve, on the defensive, but humour still bubbling in the arid desert of conversation. "Science is the only way of discovering reality. Our concepts are the result of logical deduction."

"Logic is only a brain function," I said. "Without brains, there's no logic, so logic itself doesn't exist...There you are, I've just used logic to prove that logic doesn't exist.... It's just another human idea; just a chemical reaction in the brain..."

"Can we get back to big balls and fucking?" asked Jock, stubbing out his Joint. I ignored Jock, watching Steve shake his head at my mumbo jumbo.

"Of course, logic is a brain function! It evolved to be logical, since reality is logical. Brains have to deal with reality, and reality is made up of consistent, natural laws."

"Reality isn't logical, only a certain way of thinking is logical..." I insisted.

"Rubbish!" said Steve, and then he stood up, unsteadily. "Try thinking that this foot making forceful contact with you nuts won't hurt. I bet your thinking won't make any difference to the reality..."

Grinning, Steve grabbed my coat and tried to kick me in the balls. We danced in circles under the moon like a couple of laughing maniacs. I kept my knees together as much as possible as Steve tried to put the boot in.

"The reality is my thinking!" I panted, " Pain is a thought. Pain would only exist in my nervous system and in my thoughts.... There's no pain out there in this reality of yours. Ouch! You bastard! There are *things* in the world and there are minds- the *en-soi* and the ...Get off!...the *pour soi*...and minds can never be things, no matter how hard you try. You don't know what reality is; you don't know what mind is ...."

Jock looked as though he was hoping to see some genuine violence, but he would be disappointed. Cannabis only makes you want to talk and think interesting thoughts and doesn't do you much harm. Booze on the other hand causes death and mayhem everyday of the year. Which one is illegal? What sort of logic do you call that?

I pulled away from Steve and did my hopping backwards trick again, just as rabbits don't. Jock looked on, aghast. He looked at Steve, trying to understand why he could find this spectacle so funny. I tried to explain between hops.

"You shee, Jock," I panted through my teeth, " Schteeve doeschn't believe we have fwee will, that itchs only an illushun. But I don't fink any neurotranshmitter could make me do this. Itch's got no point and brains didn't evolve to do pointless fings..."

We both ended up on the grass, chuckling like school kids, staring up into space with grins on our faces.

"Fucking nonsense!" said Jock. "I'm off!" He got up but I wouldn't let him go. I grabbed his ankle.

"How'd you like lots of beer and lots of fags?" I asked eagerly. I had a good idea.

When I got back, I saw that Nicola still had her light on. A thin shaft of light escaped from the bottom of her door. I wanted to knock on her door and to ask her to share a beer with me, but instead I lit up my last Joint and let my mind roam through thoughts, experience and feelings. Stoned, moulded to my chair, staring non-judgementally into the bare wall, I was

Buddha under the Bodhi tree, waiting for enlightenment.

Heidegger asked: "Why are there things instead of nothing?" Everything is made up of atoms, right? Atoms consist of a nucleus, electrons spin around it, neutrons and protons make up the nucleus and these are made up of quarks, 'strange', 'charm', 'top', 'bottom', 'breasts', 'gorillas bollocks' etc. Then there's anti-matter, positrons that are the *Not* of electrons... We are all made up of this stuff that makes up the universe. We are the stuff of planets and stars, stuff that doesn't think at all, stuff that doesn't have awareness of its existence, stuff that isn't even stuff! In the sub-atomic world, there's only energy, waves, probability etc. Yet put together in this combination, the universe creates *me* – meat with a mind. Through mind, the universe has become conscious through its own creation. It reflects on itself, it has become aware. It started out with the animals until it reached human beings who built upon the brains of reptiles and monkeys until they could alter reality, giving the universe direction, choice, free will in its human product! Free will evolved from nothing and our awareness must be more than what we physically are.

Why and how did the universe evolve free will? Was there an intelligence behind all this or was it just chance? Was the universe looking for fulfilment, found only in communication? Could this be found only in consciousness, intelligence that evolved from matter? Was this consciousness then corrupted by our habits and our cultures that emerged over the years of our evolution? Religion, falsity and bad faith emerged that the higher intelligence was indifferent to. It rejected its blindly worshipping 'fans', admiring the atheists, the uncertain, the ones that don't know, the ones that could rise above their tradition. Perhaps the way to God is through atheism because He wants intelligent communication, not dominance, not power. A higher intelligence wouldn't want obedience and worship; worship is embarrassing to an intelligent being; it wouldn't have a petty ego like that if it could create a universe! People throughout history have spoken the most potent bullshit. Finding God in atheism is surely no more ridiculous an idea. In fact, isn't that precisely what Kierkergaard did? He found God in an abyss of absurdity. He gave up looking for 'rules' but I must resist the lure of peace of mind. I have to have the truth!

At this moment, all I really know is that I want to make mad passionate love to Nicola, choking on an orgasm that brings forth thunder and lightning that shakes the pre-biotic soup, that creates life, amino acids, its incredible mystery …

I hear laughter in the next room; people are enjoying themselves but I'm too stoned to be jealous or bitter.

A few weeks later

There've been a couple of parties recently that I need to write about. The first one was in the Psychology department. Steve invited me along to it. Now, I must mention that I don't normally like parties very much. I've always been baffled by the compulsory physical gyrations, the intolerable noise and the fit-inducing lights that usually go with them. Conversation is banished to the peripheries where there is always some poor soul sitting in the corner with sick down his shirt.

I was determined not to be that poor soul on this occasion and to remain fairly sober. This was Steve's advice to me - the expert on human behaviour, especially female behaviour. He said that we should plan our assault carefully, synchronise our watches and agree on midnight for the first raid, when the enemy was at its most vulnerable. It was all playful stuff.

Sadly, the party didn't seem well attended and the music was turned up to make it seem like the dozen or so students there were enjoying themselves. Bowls of crisps and plates of French bread looked lifeless and unwanted. I picked up a paper plate to nestle some cheesy footballs upon it. A little pile of paper serviettes sat next to the plates, looking no less forlorn. Inanimate objects, they seem to have something to say, like the piece of paper I found in the park. Here around the crinkly edges of the plate was a reservoir of human striving for company, comfort and kindness in a very short life. That's why happy things are always depressing.

Worse than paper plates is colourful wrapping paper, birthday cakes with candles sticking out of them, old people taking photographs of children. It all does me in! I nearly abandoned Steve's advice and wanted to down a strong lager to escape these peculiar haunted feelings, but it was interesting to remain sober for a change. I could be like a bird of prey, watching the mice boldly venturing out into the open, enjoying themselves. In a minute, there will be a black shadow across the sun and 'whoosh'!...

A 'mouse' was walking my way, slightly unsteady on her paws. She looked around the table, in search of cheese. She looked at me and was grinning all over her face, mouse-like.

"I'm sure I left a drink here," she shouted above a song that had made millions, despite being based on three chords. I could smell garlic bread and that chemistry lab stench that you smell on people's breath when they have been drinking and you haven't. It's something I hadn't smelt in a long while.

"There's plenty in the kitchen," I yelled back, nodding in the appropriate direction. At this point, I knew that something had been set in motion. The coin had gone in, and the arm of the bandit given a tug. The possibilities were whirling in front of my eyes and I just had to wait for the outcome. She followed me into the kitchen. The 'Id' was clambering up my spine again, talking the obvious and shouting obscenities. 'Ego' applied the gag and tied the bugger up. We arrived at the table, groaning with an array of intoxicants.

"What are you having?" I said.

I took her all in a split second, now that the light was better. She had long legs, a beautiful full bum, breasts like unexploded bombs dropped and buried in the swamp of the male psyche. Long, sandy coloured hair fell about her delicate shoulders. You get the picture, I trust! I felt myself salivating as I poured her a vodka into a plastic cup. You remember what happened to the last female vodka drinker that I knew. If not, you haven't been paying attention. She thanked me.

I spied Steve in the epicentre, glowing with alternating colours like some crazy spook. Prisms of white light danced across him and crawled across his face like maggots. He was grinning, pointing at his watch, mouthing that I was ahead of schedule. I suppressed a laugh and turned my attention to the girl before me.

"So, you're doing Psychology, then?" I said. This is the 'nice weather for the time of year' of university. It's so boring, but everyone does it. She nodded and asked me what I was studying. (The equivalent of 'It looks like rain later on'). I told her. She seemed interested.

"I read a philosophy book once," she said.

"Have you come across the existentialists? "

"Not really," she said, leaning against the wall. I saw perspiration between her noticeable cleavage. She was wearing a white gypsy top with those dangly bits around the bust. I could see the outline of her bra beneath it. Sometimes I think that evolution has developed a special mechanism within the male eye that allows us to look at crotches, bums and breasts without the female noticing, but perhaps I'm just kidding myself. They probably know exactly what you're doing. I couldn't think of what to say, so I just pressed on.

"Would you say that 'existence comes before essence'?" I said, sensing the presence of the absurd.

"Nobody's ever asked me that before," she mocked.

"I don't beat about the bush," I said, "I just come right out with it!"

"No, it was that stuff about everything being mental...Crisp?"

"Oh yes, thanks." I took a small handful and munched them one at a time so that I could talk through them - Salt and vinegar philosophy.

"Idealism? Yes, I know a bit about it, but I'd love to hear what you think of it."

Was I making her feel good? Was I in with a chance? I needed Steve's impartial advice.

She topped up her smile with vodka and then filled it with carbohydrate. She was trying to remember the name of the book she had read. She scratched her head, shifting fronds of sandy hair, slightly heavy with sweat.

"It was by Bertrand Russell, I think. He wrote a lot about his table in it." Then she laughed.

"He had a nice table, I believe," I said. Wonderful! We were beginning to sink into the beckoning absurdity.

"He kept saying that it was hard and smooth, but not when seen under a microscope," she laughed, slapping my shoulder, enjoying the double entendre.

"And it made a rapping sound when he hit it with his knuckles," I added, making her laugh again, "Olive?"

"Thanks," she said. This was great! The rod was bending, a few clicks audible on a slowly turning reel. She scratched her head again.

"What was I saying? "

"You were going to tell me your views on the doctrine of Absolute Idealism, I think. There was a chapter about it in Russell's book," I said. Ego was screaming at Id: "Not yet! Hold fire! We're getting there!"

"Oh yes! I remember," she said, standing back and conducting her own speech, her hands like batons, spoons, screwdrivers and buckets collecting samples of air. The vodka made her points full of inconsistency and contradictions. I was really beginning to like her.

"... and so there's no way of us experiencing the *real* table, if there's a real table at all. All we can know is what goes on in our heads, which is not the same thing as matter. We might as well assume that everything is mental because we can't experience anything else. That scared me a bit and I had to stop reading the book. I don't think I really understood it, actually."

"Cheesy football?" I said, holding out a depleted bowl. She took a handful.

"I bet you don't have to watch your weight. You've got a really nice...I mean you're really slim, aren't you? I hope you don't think I'm 'objectifying' you or anything," I said.

"What do you mean?"

"Well, don't you think Feminism has gone too far? Am I a sexist because I like women's bodies?"

"It depends how you express your liking," she said, looking at me with suspicion. Steve suggested the direct approach. It works for him so why shouldn't it work for me, just once? I tugged on the rod, turning the reel; my heart began to beat fast.

"Would you like to come back with me? .... Please?"

The bombs were released; the nose was down into the dive. The first fruit was thumping to a halt -a lemon! No good! I saw the full comprehension of my intentions staring back at me from her eyes, her two mirrors like lasers burning out my brains, turning me to stone. How many times had she been in this situation? How many times did she discover that she could never have a friendly chat with someone, a friendly bit of fun without the man wanting to ravish her? All this came out of her eyes and I saw myself in there, in her consciousness, being processed, categorised and destroyed. It was too late for an apology. The rod snapped and the line spun out loosely, the 'one that got away'.

"Excuse me, I want to dance..." she said, and walked off.

I watched her moving again beneath the flashing lights, laughing again, smiling again. What was she laughing at? Her genes were doing their work, seeking out the dominant males to mate her, rejecting the lower ranks. Her bottom shone blue for a moment, as blue as a fertile monkey's being proffered to the ones that dare - the fighters, the big, muscled ones, the one's that have more than their fair share of resources. And I knew what had frightened her about what she had read. What if those big men that seek her out were all of her own imagination? What if the sexual power she has is just an illusion and there were no real men out there at all? Her genes, her vanity, her taunting sexuality couldn't take that!... Sorry, this is all crap! I'm just bitter and twisted. I'll tell you about the other party...

The Philosophy party had no florescent bottoms, but the music was more comprehensible. It was panpipe music from the Andes. One or two of the younger lecturers had turned up, hoping to hit it off with some young flesh, despite being married with children.

Once again, the sad paper plates were out. There was even a cheerful trifle, wobbling like a clown that no one was paying any attention to. A red coat with silver buttons. I saw the effort that had gone into it - that primitive part of us that shares and exchanges food to create peace between us. Steve's eyes scanned the lecture hall.

"There's not much to be getting on with here, " he said. It was hard to tell whether he was being serious or not, but I felt irritated by him. He liked chasing women, but what satisfaction did he ever get out of it? I don't think he's really after any real 'connection', any real 'transcendence' through sex. It's all just a game to him; a game he has to win. Women aren't 'mystical' to him. He's such an empiricist, such a practical, cause and effect, 'Psychology is a science' type of bastard that he's forgotten how to feel. I feel too much, love women too much, but can't quite reach them. 'Women' is my religion. They are like God to me; just like God, in fact. They never answer your prayers, they never yield to compassion; they are beyond understanding; they show no mercy. Yet I go on worshipping them, no matter how indifferent or unaware they are of my torment. I go on sacrificing my life fluids on my stomach's altar in the name of women.

Saturday Morning

I've just opened a letter and just couldn't believe my eyes. It was from Anny. She wants to see me! I can't think why, or how she tracked me down. A mixture of outrage and pleasure got thrown together like an oil slick on a bathing beach. What trap was she setting me, and why? The past is dead, only smoke remains where there was once a fire, smoke that gets caught in the breeze and eventually joins the paradise of non-existence! Why is this ghost trying to haunt me? She's answering my letter way too late!

I've been sitting here for hours, watching and listening, just existing, paying attention to what it's like to exist. I look at all the things around me that don't move; that have no sensations or thoughts. I've learned a lot in my life. I've learned that we had primate ancestors, (some of which had big balls) and that it's just our genes that want us to have sex, using us to replicate ourselves. I can accept all this stuff, because clever people have worked it all out and it's better than believing in a load of nonsense like Noah's ark and all that, but I have no experience of human prehistory and no real contact with my DNA. They just feel like human concepts to me, things that aren't really real – just ideas. I have this ghostly feeling of being alive in a ghostly world with other ghosts, where nothing is quite real or convincing. If only I could stop thinking! Thoughts stretch out endlessly, going on and on and on, pointlessly.

I don't trust 'facts' or the thoughts that make facts 'true'. Every 'fact' has its denial. There's a god; there's no god; we are innately good; we are innately bad; society is 'out there', controlling us; society is in our heads; we live in a meritocracy; we live under a Ruling class... How do I choose between all these ideas? If I decide to believe in something, I then realise that I've only decided to 'believe' so that I can have an identity. To believe in something is really an admission that you *don't* believe in something. Believing in something always comes with it the recognition that its contradiction could be true. I don't want to find a 'belief' that I can't fully believe in; I want real experience and at the moment, negativity, negation is my experience-*not this, not that*. Sometimes it's "Yes! That!" when I see a beautiful girl or hear Bach, but both can only remain outside my experience. I can't love the beautiful girl and I'll never understand the mind of Bach. I thought that understanding tramps might be a bit easier, but I'm not so sure! We're all something more than the stereotype we try to find ourselves in. We're all unrealised and unresolved. Jock defines himself as a 'Not'. Like me, he's *not* a social success, *not* a respectable member of society, *not* a person who holds the mainstream values so he's not free after all. So long as we live with 'others', with society, he can't be free. What do I mean by free? I mean 'real', unconditioned, not false!

Despite my outrage, I feel almost exhilarated that I've existed in her memory for so long! I was a long-term neural pathway, a trace, a connection. Her physiological reactions kept me alive. I exist for someone else, not just myself. A pop star, a musician, a 'great person' exists in millions of brains. I'm not sure that I could take that intensity of existence.

Just one person almost overwhelms me. I basked in the painful ecstasy of it all. "I am, I exist, I think, therefore I am, I am because I think; why do I think? What if I gave up thinking? Would I still 'be'?" I get up and go for a walk. Here I am, existing in this particular place at this particular time, strangely detached, out of context. I'm naked, unlike those that don't realise, that think that they just 'are', that they just appear in the world, go out for a curry or a beer, watch the football, wriggle in their small day-to-day controversies. I'm different in that I know I'm exactly the same as they are! They just *are*, competent, comprehending, complete, confident, conspicuous – they pull women, put in earrings, grow moustaches, use mobile phones, get well paid jobs. But me, *I don't think, therefore I am a moustache!* (If you think that's daft, it's from Sartre's *Nausea*. Read it yourself if you don't believe me!) How can I give up this self, this awareness? It's always here to torment me. Hell isn't other people- it's yourself (or the illusion of self). You can escape others but there's no escape from yourself, (unless the Buddhists are right).

Sunday

I have x-ray eyes. I can see right through everyone and everything. Everything is transparent and wraith-like. Nothing matters, there are no 'facts' to discover, no reason for living, no adequate reason for suicide, no morals, no god, no absolutes, no rational choice between conflicting values. Solidity is an illusion, no solid real things in ideas; they shift and move dangerously, like sand dunes in the desert. I stand beneath the desert sun, waiting....

I went to see Steve, but he seemed 'stand-offish', like another person. The unbridgeable nothingness between us had grown wider, as it does with everyone, every relationship or friendship. I had disturbed him in the middle of some serious study. Seeing those open text- books, his A4 pad of paper, his little environment supporting his self- image, it made me want to laugh. He was taking his degree seriously again.

"I've got to work harder and drink less," he announced.

"I see...so, what brought this on? Anything to do with gorilla's bollocks?"

Steve adopted the persona of a socially created being, someone dedicated to integrity, to service, professionalism and no longer to absurdity.

"There's a practical base to what I'm studying," said Steve. "It's fundamentally about helping other people. That's why I want to be a psychologist. I don't want to doss through my degree. I've just got to *do* something with my life."

"But Steve," I said, "Psychology is a waste of time."

Steve awaited my explanation with a peeved expression on his face.

"It's shit because it tries to treat consciousness as if it acts in lawful ways!"

"Not that again! We've been through this before. Consciousness acts in lawful ways to match the lawful ways of nature," he said, wearily.

"We broke free of natural laws by becoming conscious. Nothing stops us from doing what the hell we like. There are no laws of human nature really; existence comes before essence, that's why psychology is rubbish."

"This is all nonsense, Antoine," said Steve, irritated, outraged, " This Cartesian split between body and mind has been solved. It was a big mistake. Metaphysics is extinct."

"You lot just pretend that all there is to humans is 'behaviour' because you can't face the inexplicable. Because you have no idea what consciousness really is, you have all these clever ways to explain it away. You're like those physicists who tell us that the universe began with a big bang. At one point there was *absolutely nothing*, then there were the laws of physics that caused an explosion. So where did the damned laws of physics come from then, eh? Isn't the sudden appearance of the laws of physics out of nothingness a breach of the laws of physics?"

"Not my area of expertise I'm afraid..."

"Mind has no cause either; it's not body and it's not behaviour. None of your words will capture it. If we're just physical things, how can a physical thing know that it's just a physical thing? If it knows it's just a physical thing, it can't just be a physical thing. It doesn't add up..."

"You're so full of contradiction! On the one hand you're an atheist and on the other, you're embracing mumbo jumbo. No wonder you're confused!"

"Confusion is honesty. Certainty is bollocks. That's Voltaire. "

Steve sighed. I can see ambition growing within him. He wants a career in his subject. He'll make a great psychologist. He'll discover that if you treat monkeys really badly in their infancy, they'll grow up to be disturbed monkeys. He'll notice that people are more likely to do something if they are rewarded for it or if someone in authority tells them to do it, that sometimes we're aggressive and sometimes not, that children learn the language they hear and as they get older, they are capable of more complex thought. Well bugger me! People get paid for this!

Steve didn't accept anything I said and wanted me to leave so that he could get on with his work. I told Steve to learn to be an ambulance driver if he really wanted to help others. Steve had an intellect that I didn't have. Steve had an ego that bounced back from absurdity. The strings dangled from above; I traced them up to the ceiling and further on into the infinite universe. He wasn't ready to fall at the feet of existence. I have to leave the subject of Anny's letter for another time. She wanted to meet me again. What on earth for?

"You've got to care about *something*," said Steve, exasperated. He rolled a cigarette, his fingers fumbling slightly with agitation.

"Authenticity!" I shot back. Steve just barked out a laugh of mild contempt.

"There's no authenticity in staying permanently drunk and lazy."

"Not according to Sartre. Getting pissed is just as valid as being the bloody prime minister!" I said.

"You've got your views and I've got mine. I'm not an existentialist, I'm a humanist."

"Sartre reckoned they went together..."

"Will you shut up about Sartre! And stop quoting all the time. It's boring! You think psychology is crap. Well, as it happens, I feel the same about philosophy. Psychology turned a load of waffle into something that could actually be used!" said Steve, sneering.

"I think Philosophy is crap too. It's just a game with words. Words never say anything, except how clever the person is who's using them."

"Why the hell are you studying it then?"

"Many reasons. To get out of working, to increase my chances of having a bonk. It's the starting point for my search. I'm searching for the truth!"

Steve inhaled on his roll-up and blew a thin stream of smoke with an audible force. I watched the smoke disperse in the air with a heightened awareness. He didn't want to hear about searches. It was such a waste of time.

"I'd better let you get on with your work then," I said, feeling slightly guilty that I too wasn't delving into the deep fountain of human knowledge. It isn't really that I'm lazy; it's just that 'facts' strike me as arrogant. Words, words, words, invented by other minds, sculptured into impressive creations, but I didn't make them. I just have to accept their superiority. Intellects tower above you, looking down upon us scum from their snooty, clever noses!

"I am a bit busy…." said Steve, indicating the books and papers on his desk. The roll-up started to disintegrate in his saucer ashtray.

"How big are a Gibbon's bollocks?" I asked. Steve grinned reluctantly, but he wasn't sure. He would have to look it up and make it relevant to the ordered world of psychology. A bell rings and a dog salivates – Big deal! A little boy wants to fuck his mum. Crap!

Friendships are a bit of a hit and miss affair, I feel! We pretend to be in the same place, to see the world in the same way but it's just something that we use to support ourselves. I'll approve of you if you approve of me; I'll give you a favourable image of yourself if you'll do the same for me. Two people don't really connect; they are just using each other. Steve thinks he's 'outgrown' me but he's really just turned tail in the face of uncomprehending existence.

Monday

I must admit I did withhold certain facts when I wrote about that beautiful girl I danced with. I had, in fact, joined the ballroom dancing society, much to my embarrassment. I thought that this would definitely be the place to meet some babes. Well, I went back again and made a contract with my genes, that if I don't pull this time, they can go head banging again in the lethal pink bouncy castle. They agreed to my terms. The race was on between me and Steve, even though we'd never said it, but one of us had to 'pull' soon.

Anyway, I awaited my turn to dance with this total babe! Putting my hands around her was like skydiving, like putting your arms into a trunk load of money! I looked at her in the eyes as we danced, me clumsily, her proficiently. I waited for a chat-up line that didn't sound too false, determined to avoid the 'what are you studying?' nonsense.

"So what you are studying then?" she said to me. I was shocked.

"Philosophy," I said with apologetic tones.

"Oh really? I'm doing psychology," she said.

"Psychology? I didn't see you at that party. I would have remembered. Do you know Steve - Steve Smith? He's a friend of mine."

"Oh, I certainly do! He's nice. Feet firmly on the ground!" she said. I wanted to wipe that interested look off her face.

"In the sub-atomic world, there is no firm ground for your feet."

"Sorry?"

"Nothing. So, you like Steve, do you?" I asked.

"He's very intelligent! He works hard. I think he's going to get a 'first'".

"Do you want me to put in a good word for you?" I said.

"Oh no, don't! I always get my man!"

The music stopped. She smiled with great affection, like giving me a big present in pretty paper then seeing that the tag had another's name on it. Perhaps she had something to do with Steve's change of attitude. I thought men were supposed to put friendship before females.

"It was so nice to meet you. My name's Rachel by the way."

She shook my hand. It was sporting of her, to thank the loser for the contest. She fancied my best friend, what a vicious cow! Well, I wasn't going to feed his ego. I wasn't going to congratulate him.

"Hey, Rachel. There's a girl I met at the Psychology party - long blonde hair, nice....Do you know who I mean? "

I hadn't let go of her hand and those vital seconds had passed where it was no longer legitimate or appropriate to be hanging on to it. The 'Weird' sign had gone up in her mind. I let her have it back but could still feel its imprint in mine, still warm. She didn't know her name but had seen her around. She had a reputation for being an 'easy lay'. It seems I can't even score with the one's who are giving it away!

This made the genes restless, like unfed horses in their stables. They kicked at the barn doors, splintering wood; sex and anger burned on the same bonfire. It was time for me to honour the agreement. It was late, but time enough for some Dutch courage and a trip to the massage parlour that never closed, a different one from my first visit. This time my purchase was dull witted and bored in her work. She was all right to look at though, as long as she kept her mouth shut. I examined her with the meticulousness of a GP. It was that old question again: Isn't it funny how a rude thought can change the shape of your cock? I was philosophising with an erection - not easy! I mean, what *is* it that we find so exciting? The vagina is a 'nothing' in reality. It's a void, a space, a hole! But between legs like these, 'the hole is greater than the sum of its parts'.

"I'd like to do it from behind," I said, decisively. She turned over obediently and put her bum in the air, one eye stared up at me with indifference. Something stirred in my guts, a flash of arousal and understanding, as if I was looking at the secrets of the universe through the back door. I put on the condom, like putting a dead snake into a body bag (you know.... rigour mortis.... oh never mind!) The universe spun in my head as I thrust with the unthinking joy of an animal, pushing in deeper, feeling myself disappear and melt away again, driven by a mysterious force of transcendence where orgasm is the only answer to all the questions. My mind suddenly exploded into a tortured, primal scream, my genes rewarding me with a cocktail of chemicals, and it was all over rather quickly again. The big bang that began the universe slowly solidified into planets and stars. I fell back into reality and my precious genetic material reached its usual resting place, in the bin liner.

"Don't you find this degrading?" I heard myself say, as I struggled to get one foot back into my underpants, hopping around like a demented Flamingo.

"Do you?"

"Yes. I think I do, but I don't know why."

"Well, don't do it then," she said. Logical and intelligent enough! Her answers were monosyllabic, as if she were in a police interview. She *was* what she did. Her manner, her look, she *was* a prostitute. She had cast herself in the drama of life.

"I wish I could stop myself, but it's a drug. I get the need." I said, apologetically.

She said nothing, just shrugged. I wanted to tell her that I was fully aware that I was nothing to her - just another punter. It suddenly occurred to me why some prostitutes just get people who want to talk. I wanted to talk now, too. I wanted to explain my search, my questioning, my mental anguish and bridge the gaps between male and female and the thousand and one things that separate one mind from another, but she would not want to know.

"It's the sordidness that I like," I said, "It's like a kind of defiance."

She pulled on her jeans; I listened to the swishing sound as they covered her arse that I had known.

"Your sordidness is my living," she said.

"It's never 'love' then?" I said, embarrassed. She laughed like a cannon shot, her face etched with cynicism.

"Love?" she laughed. She took out a lipstick from a small handbag and began to paint her face. I watched her disappear beneath a fresh mask, ready to be the fantasy of the next client.

"I wish we could understand all this; don't you? Why do you think we're here? You know? What do you think the purpose of life is? Can I buy you a drink? I'd like to hear everything about your life from as far back as you can remember. Be as honest as..."

"If you want to talk, you'll have to pay again," she said, putting her bra on.

"Are you a prostitute or a psychiatrist? Which one has the more valuable social role?"

She didn't know what I meant but she told me to piss off. Perhaps she was insulted by the word 'psychiatrist'. Was she disgusting or was she just a member of the low life? Was I disgusting? Was I just being honest about my inexplicable need to 'have' a woman, or was I just pathetic? Just a loser? Why did I have to pay everyone before they would talk to me – tramps, prostitutes, counsellors! My genes satisfied, I skipped home, full of joy, because there was nothing to be joyful about; it was absurdity and the unanswerable that made me joyful.

Tuesday

'Helping others' is Steve's ambition. When you have an ego that insists on helping others in order to justify itself, it will seek out the sick and wounded and subject them to 'cures' that they never asked for. Some people want to make money, others want to 'save souls'; there's a comparable conniving careerist background to all this!

Do people that 'help others' do it because they are 'good' or are they doing it because they have ambition? The ambulance drivers, social workers, people who 'help' - are they doing it to escape the absurd? Behind their altruism, is there a soul that hopes to please God or an action that will please an ego? Is there really any such thing as 'good'? I've looked for it within me but don't see it. I started going to the Ethics lectures because of this. There are some philosophers who think that there's no such thing as 'altruism', that all acts of goodness always benefit us in some way. I don't know what to believe again!

I walked through the market today and I listened to the street sellers. "C'mon ladies, only five pound. I'm giving it away today..."

He slapped a lump of red meat with white fat around it, grinning, asking the 'lads' what it reminded them of. I felt sick again. He was right; we *are* meat, smelly soft lubricating meat. Beautiful women go to the toilet and wipe their bums; blood oozes from their fleshy holes every month; beautiful women digest food and have bad breath in the morning. It's all an illusion! Beneath the skin are blood and guts, fluids and coils of pipes. Hammering into my head, the need to understand existence, as imperceptibly, my meat decays each passing year.

I reached Hines' door again. He looked even less pleased to see me than before, but at least he recognised me. How could he forget? This time a chair had been cleared of papers and his desk was scrupulously tidy. Steve would have called this 'reaction-formation'. I sat down, a chuckle threatening already. He had my essay in his hand. It was odd seeing your own words in the grip of another's consciousness. I wish he could have dropped the pose and laugh about what happened last time.

"Well, I gave it a pass," he said, eyeing me with suspicion, "but I can't say I approve of the unconventional language."

I remembered, and felt childish. He looked at me again and read from my essay.

"All attempts to reduce human consciousness to either conditioned responses or to neurological firings is ....*bollocks*...." he said with distaste.

He expected some sort of explanation. I felt silly.

"I admit, passion ran away with me," I said.

Hines sat down, constantly adjusting his bifocals, as if hoping he was mistaken.

"Logical positivists would find your statement meaningless, since 'bollocks' is merely a crude word to represent male genitalia. There's no reason why 'bollocks' should symbolically represent that which is worthless or despicable," he said dryly.

"My essay was about free will, not linguistics."

"Hmm...." Hines adjusted his tie. "Apart from the odd language, there were some reasonable points, if a little anecdotal!" he conceded, bitterly.

"Life is one big anecdote, though isn't it? It's not something that we decide to do after reasoned debate and research," I said.

Hines looked at me again. He seemed to be wondering what sort of idiot he had in his office, and when he should expect the demand for money. A pencil twitched between his skeletal fingers, a familiar ritual, no doubt not entirely unconnected with unconscious masturbation.

"Your essay seems to reveal you as something of a Nihilist, " he said.

"Everything is crap. Sartre said the same thing but more eloquently." I replied.

A baffled silence emerged between us, pregnant with hostility and confusion. Hines took off his glasses. Steve would have said that this contained unconscious significance- he didn't want to look at me. But, of course, *he* didn't want to be my friend anymore! I was thinking like a sulky child.

"I'm wondering...." said Hines. "I'm wondering if you don't have some psychological issues that need working through."

I sensed his indifference beneath the tact.

"You think I'm bonkers?"

"No. That's not what I said..."

"All the greatest thinkers were mad, weren't they? -- Nietzsche, Leibnitz..."

"Not so much 'mad'. In your case, more 'bitter', perhaps."

I shrugged slightly. I didn't mean to, but I felt my shoulders move.

"I'm like that bloke who pushed the rock up the hill...." I said.

"Sisyphus," said Hines.

"Condemned to an eternity of pointless activity."

"But Sisyphus was happy in doing it. Read Camus."

"Why?" I asked. Did I detect a faint gasp in my voice? "Was it because he couldn't see how pointless his life was or because he was happy with the pointlessness of it?"

Hines let his fingers sway gently in the breeze of his thoughts. He threatened to smile.

"Sisyphus is just like any other mountaineer. He did it for the exercise and the view from the top. He just had an extra heavy piece of equipment to take with him."

A vague smile broke through, revealing dentures. White gleaming pearls in the face of gradual decay.

"Sartre and Camus say there's *nothing*. We're the only species that can see it. It's hard to take anything seriously when you know there's fundamentally nothing."

Hines gave the impression of a smile again. His eyes looked old. He was close to death. I wanted to ask him what it felt like. Was there panic, regret, anger? But I knew a ten year old would ask me the same question. I focused on Hines' socks. I couldn't bear his old face decaying before me. He had holes in his socks and his feet seemed huge in his eccentrically scruffy shoes.

"Why the obsession with Sartre? He's not the be all and end all. Read some other philosophers."

"I just have this suspicion that it's all a joke, a con- words and books. I read a short story by Chekov. It was about a man who spent fifteen years in prison for a bet"

"I've read it. "

" – And he spent all that time reading everything he could lay his hands on..."

"I know. "

" -And in the end he thought everything was pointless and crap. In the end all we are capable of is words. We're all going to die. There's no point in anything! He couldn't be bothered to take his two million pound winnings!"

"Some people take their insights a little too seriously."

"I've looked at eastern philosophy to escape 'conceptual thought' and found out that 'the truth can't be told in words', but I start wondering if that's just words too. There's no point if there's no point in the end."

"You mean no God?"

"I don't even see the point of God and eternal life. What am I going to do for eternity? After a billion years I'd have all the pleasures I could take, all the dreary, grovelling worship that I could stomach! An eternity of boredom seems worse than complete annihilation."

Hines stood up and stretched his back with a sigh and mild discomfort. It was my cue to leave.

"There's no point in dwelling on pointlessness either, is there? What insight can be found in being a misery? Sartre himself warned against confusing disenchantment with the truth. It's not all bad you know!"

What is truth then? Is it the opposite of disenchantment - happiness? Can happiness ever be the final answer or just a compromise or a cop-out? Disenchantment always seems to be more realistic- more true. The bison under the tiger's claws, the mouse in the cat's jaws - that's what's 'true'. The truth is *suffering* – the first noble truth of Buddhism. Suffering is better than nothing.

I walked towards the park once again. It had become my favourite haunt. Jock was elsewhere today. I was glad. I just wanted to sit and watch. My mind was in a whirl. I didn't know what I even felt, let alone what I believed in. I just let it happen. I saw no reason to be involved. I would be nihilistic; if a murderer were to come and stab me, so be it. I would accept the end of my life without emotion or regret. I sat down on the bench, watching people and everything around me, the trees, the kids kicking a ball, the grass. I stared at the huge tree in front of me wondering how old it was, wondering if old men with Top Hats and ladies in full skirts and bustles had chatted beneath it. They must have done. I was the main character in Sartre's *Nausea*. Fact and fiction were merging alarmingly. I hoped it wasn't a breach of copyright to look at a tree!

That tree was very, very old, it held the past in its sap and in its branches. The silent past stared out from it, without comment. It was a blind man with waving arms. I watched its huge roots plunge into the soil, like a huge penis raping the earth. I could understand what that pipe smoking French man was saying now. Why did it do this? How could it be explained? A tree itself isn't just the word 'tree'. A 'tree' is this *very* thing in front of me! It's a monster- an inescapable frozen mass of atoms that can't explain themselves. Naked existence hides behind our words and when you see through the words, see through the illusion that words are the reality, the truth of existence jumps out at you! Things exist, including yourself without any true reason or explanation! But now my consciousness of the tree and that thing itself melted and merged together, and I felt something slipping away – my resistance and my distress. Something familiar about myself was dissolving and dying. The tree had no ego and didn't worry about existing. I was becoming the tree! And I hadn't even had a spliff!

Wednesday

I sketched out my idea for a PhD I'd never do, the connection between Buddhism and existentialism. Sartre says 'Hell is other people' but the Buddhists say there *are* no 'other people' – everything is one; there's no division or separation. Yet both are saying that identities are false. If only I could be a Buddhist! I want to but absurdity kicks in every time! I don't want to join a 'club' - 'I can't face the reality of death' club. That's all religion is. Every religion.

I found that Anny had sent another letter. I threw it away without even opening it. Revenge is sweet, but I wished I could show more indifference, like a horse swishing flies from its arse. A lingering curiosity taunted me. The old self had sneaked back again. Would I ever have such an experience again? It was delicious to have no identity- delicious and terrifying, psychotic but authentic. Free from 'ego', free from the nightmare of self.

I actually attended all the lectures and seminars that I was supposed to today. There was nothing else to do. I wish I hadn't bothered. How tedious to discuss how Marx inverted Hegel's view on historical change, especially when that blonde has such shapely, pert breasts. My genes are at it again! Why couldn't they shut up for one minute and let me get on with my life? How beautiful she looks, sitting there; her tiny hand grasping her 'biro' in such a funny way. I don't know how she did it, but somehow she managed to twist the subject under discussion to feminism. She was always doing this, complaining that Philosophy had been an exclusive male club for too long. A change of genitalia was vital to the advancement of knowledge and understanding.

The seminar was no better. She was off again, confident and purposeful with a cause. Once again, the bottom line seemed to be that poor old women are oppressed! I think there ought to be a game where one group mentions any subject under the sun and the other group relates it to issues of gender and race – table tennis, the weather, Geology…. You name it.

Now, I have a confession to make. I think that feminism is a load of crap and just another way that some people (Women), grasp at an identity. There is no need for a special kind of justice for the female sex. Justice does not have genitalia. What I think is that men and women have different genes. Men's genes are loud and selfish and are always shouting: " Let's fuck!" but women's genes whisper more and say things like "Ooh, babies,

babies!". This makes biological sense to me. My genes have never whispered "Ooh, babies!" to me. It's a division of labour you see. They reason that their job is to get in there and get that egg, leaving the female genes in charge of production. When women moan about men, they are just condemning what a man is, they are just moaning about biology and evolution. But then I come across a contradiction, of course! I find myself negating the view that we have free will, since feminism is based on the idea that we are *free* from biological influences and it's our *culture* that shapes us. All differences are socially constructed, they say. I can't help it! I still say it's crap! I say that consciousness has unlimited freedom but biology doesn't. We can't ignore the genes completely. We are free, but free within a prison. We are not free to deny the truth. I hope that makes sense. No, it doesn't really! It's all too confusing and contradictory. Sexism, Racism, Blasphemy-'formulas' to replace experience, moulds to shape our thoughts, barriers to clamp down on real feelings, badges to create identities. I just have to poke, prod and provoke the new orthodoxy. I have to negate until I can find the truth within me!

….Sorry to interrupt again, but I just wanted to mention that the views expressed by the central character are not necessarily those held by its author. The latter is much more together and he is only trying to show how a young student's mind might work – you know, like *Catcher in the Rye*. When some nutter kills a famous pop star with a copy of *my* book in his pocket, then I'll know I've made it!

On my way back to my grotty room, I went into a big shop called 'Athena' and browsed through the posters. There had to be something that appealed to me or reflected my 'inner core'. Definitely not bloody Madonna, not a woman scratching her bare arse on a tennis court, not some science fiction character, not a cartoon, not a car, nor a 'legalise it' poster. I couldn't find anything that I liked. Even the big- titted woman striking a pose and looking a bit angry did nothing for me. I found one of trees and bought it. There was no glamour, no ideology behind it, just trees. Just a bloody tree, existing, reaching for the skies, rooted in the ground, existing without a thought. I took it back and blue-tacked it to the wall. I could almost hear a sigh of relief – at last! If there's one thing I remember from my experience, it's that 'emptiness' is not the same as 'nothingness', Buddhists and existentialists don't quite meet eye to eye. If I wanted to avoid another three years of work, I might just have to do that PhD! The poster stuck out, bright colours against bareness, but soon it would be background, melting and merging with the ordinary – just like a new hi-fi, just like a new woman. I wish we could experience life afresh every day, where every pint was perfect, every kiss a thrill, every touch a shock of pleasure, every meeting with another, full of wit and joy. There was a knock on my door. It made me jump. Who knocks on my door? It was a rare event. I jumped up and opened it. It was Nicola. She stood there holding a note. She had her glasses on, making her look vulnerable. She had tight jeans on. She handed me a note.

"A woman wanted to know where you were. She gave me this to give to you."

I took the note and tore open the envelope and immediately screwed it up and dropped it on the floor. Nicola shrugged her shoulders with a shy laugh.

"I see!" she said.

"The past is dead," I said, "but sometimes its ghosts come back to haunt you."

"I'm…. I'm afraid I suggested she came back later."

"I'd better go out again, then," I said.

She smiled and suddenly I saw flowers and hills and sky in her face. Not just sexual lust, a yearning, a need to protect, hold, stroke her dark hair. I never did get the courage to ask her to go for a drink. Instead of passion and joy, we had exchanged as much as coins for the phone, some milk and she'd asked me if I had a bicycle pump, which I hadn't. I never saw her other than in the corridor. I suddenly felt brave enough to test fate and chance. What could I lose?

"Nicola.... I was wondering..."

"Yes?"

"I was wondering if you would like to go for a drink sometime."

"Oh..." she said. She need not have said anything else. Her face said it all - a touch of embarrassment, a hint of guilt, a splash of difficulty, "I've got such a lot of work on at the moment. Maybe later on."

"Okay, maybe later on." I said. Life is always 'later on'.

I picked up the screwed up note and read it. She had something 'very important' to tell me. There was a phone number for me to ring. I left my room, locked it and made my way to the phone booths. I reluctantly rang the number. It rang several times before the phone was picked up. It was a tired, exhausted voice, a voice that had been stretched and strained to the limit.

"What do you want?" I said. I felt like Jock, being hassled by strangers.

"Don't put down the phone," she half warned, half pleaded. It was odd hearing her again.

"Can we meet?" she said.

"Why?"

"I don't want to tell you on the 'phone."

"I don't want to meet...."

"You give me no choice then. I've got a three-year-old child. Your child."

"What?"

Silence - then a noise; a human noise, a child noise. She was a liar.

"I don't believe you," I said.

"I knew you wouldn't, that's why I wanted to meet, and for you to meet him."

"I don't believe you".

"You'll have to when the Child Support Agency get in contact with you. I need money. I can't work. I'm on state benefits but they're going to cut it unless I name the father."

"I'm not the father."

"A DNA test will prove that you are."

"After my blood again?" I sneered.

"Aren't you interested in seeing your son?"

"No, because you're lying. Why didn't you tell me before?"

"Because you were a useless human being. I didn't want you to be involved, but I can't cope now. All my savings have gone and my benefit hardly covers food. You've got to face up to reality...."

"Reality?"

"Something you've never been willing to take notice of."

"Maybe we have different ideas of what that is," I said.

"From where I'm standing, it's nappies and poverty."

"And you want me to have some of it..."

"I told you, I want you to give me some money."

"I don't believe you!"

"Look...." She spluttered. "Matthew! Stop it! Stop it!"

There was the cry of a toddler.

"If you want to see the child that you're going to contribute towards you'll have to ring me back. I've got to go now. Goodbye."

The phone went dead. What kind of sub-plot was this? Had the writer of life completely run out of ideas? It felt as though Sisyphus had just dropped the rock on his foot. I felt as though my genes were all laughing at me. They'd escaped at last and avoided the rubber wall and the chemical death. They'd found a way! I was strangely proud! Anny, for one so in contact with reality seemed to be a little slow in realising that students are not renowned for their disposable income.

I can't believe that all the billions of people in the world are the result of a 'fumble' and a 'hump'. In the high rise buildings of New York, the lowly mud huts of some pygmy tribe, the oppressed political regimes of the world, everyone was 'at it', 'putting it in' and grunting, then nine months later, another unique person *'born between the urine and the faeces'* as Tertullian romantically pondered. Complete arseholes and Einstein had the same basic ingredients, the same journey into this weird globe, spinning around an insignificant star in the infinite universe. What is the point? What is the ultimate purpose? Surely it can't be for nothing! I'm not such an idiot to think I'm the only person to think such things – perhaps even the reversed baseball capped, ear-ringed football supporter must have taken a moment to think for a second: "Does it really, actually matter if England loses? Is this not just really a load of nonsense?"- Grown men kicking an inflated pig's bladder around a patch of grass and then some great all night celebration and an overwhelming national triumph because the bladder went between two posts more often than the other two posts up the other end?

There's a certain nobility in truth and the brute facts of nature that 'happiness' cannot provide. Me, a father, the creator of another human being? I feel like God in the garden of bloody Eden! Me, a father! I'm surprised my sperms knew what to do! Mind you, they'd had plenty of practice, plenty of excursions to understand the general plan. They'd had many years of daily fire drills. Like dropping a bomb on Moscow, the genuine attack must have come as a shock following a period of disbelief. I didn't think, just allowed these feelings to exist. But they're still not whispering "Ooh, babies", more like "You old dog, you..."

Monday?

I spent the rest of the evening in motionless silence, thinking about my son that I'd never met. Something unfamiliar within me 'cared' but that feeling was just a nugget of gold sunk in countless accumulations of lies, nonsense and deceit. I reached in to retrieve it, only to withdraw my hand caked in excrement. The thought of caring for someone was intriguing.

The knock on the door didn't sound like Nicola's. Steve walked in, all friendly and forgiving.

"Sorry about my bad mood, mate. It was the time of the month."

"No harm done. We all have these mad, irrational moments of trying to make something of our lives."

Steve stood, hands on hips, grinning and confident. He was dying to tell me something.

"I've pulled!" he announced. I felt an instant childish jealousy hit me. I wanted to sock him one.

"You lucky bastard," I said, with a 'ladish' smile.

"Rachel. She's a knock out, man! We nearly got it together last night, but you know how thin these walls are. She was scared she'd let rip."

"How very thoughtful of her."

He did not change his 'Batman' stance. The material of his dazzling blue T-shirt seemed to be flowing downwards like a serene waterfall, free from all cares. I envied the bugger and wished I could accept myself as much as he could. I wish I knew *what* I should learn to accept or like about myself. He bent over, preening himself in my mirror. If 'pulling' was such an everyday event for him, as he had led me to believe, then why did he look so particularly triumphant on this occasion? Surely the bastard wasn't 'in love'...

"Do you want to get pissed?"

"Thought you'd never ask."

We had both been having adventures and had much to talk about. Steve was not particularly amazed by my experience in the park. He doesn't believe that introspection is any basis for knowledge. He doesn't mind talking about existentialism as long as he's not expected to take it seriously. I think he realises that I don't take anything seriously. Steve's only interested in 'facts'. He's not interested in all this 'shadows in the caves' crap, as he puts it. I didn't feel any need to argue with him. Opinions are amusing little things. I told him about my phone call. He found this more interesting.

"What are you going to do?" he said.

"It all depends upon whether or not I have any free will."

"On this occasion, you do."

"I could do nothing."

"Could you marry her?"

I spat a mouthful of beer out over the table, extinguishing Steve's smelly roll-up in the plastic 'Fosters' ashtray.

"Probably not...." said Steve pulling the tobacco pouch from his jeans pocket. He sat back, all casual, his mind rummaging around in Rachel's knickers but his attention fully on our conversation. It took a real intellectual to accomplish such a feat.

"These aren't real choices," I said. "They've got society's boot behind them, ready to kick my arse. I 'm forced to make the 'right' choice."

"You could take off, before the DHSS catch up with you, but you'd never see your son."

"If free will is an illusion, what am I destined to do?"

"I've got no idea, mate."

"But shouldn't science be able to predict the outcome if I have no free will?"

"The illusion of free will is so great that we might as well act as if it really exists," said Steve. "It's impossible to identify all those variables that are making you act. There are just too many."

I didn't want to argue. This dilemma was exquisite. It felt like something real was happening in my life. I wanted to hang on to the deadlock and eventually make my own decision, not what society demanded of me. Things looking like the shadow of answers began to hover in front of my eyes. Walking away from responsibility was more of a cliché than an act of free will, perhaps. Responsibility seemed like something real. We carried on drinking, talking through various topics, both serious and absurd. Eventually Steve began to laugh.

"Are you really going to go through with the Jock thing?"

"Yes."

"Can I come to it?"

"Only if you go halves on the beer and fags."

Steve agreed to that, grinning. He got up and went to get another drink.

Tuesday

You see, it doesn't seem to me that authenticity gets you much, yet I'm committed to it. It's better to be a con artist or to talk bullshit. Modern artists can splat paint on canvas and sell it for thousands of pounds. Some posh gallery once displayed a pile of tyres, a row of bricks and a tin of excrement and called it art. Well, here's my shit, readers! There's meaning and significance in this unmade bed of a novel, in this dead-sheep-in-formaldehyde of my inner experience! I know you're supposed to empathise with the central character, but you can take it or leave it! Understand me or sod off! I don't care! I've never hit it off with girls or publishers. Rejection is the worst experience in the world, but rejection is what we have to live with, isn't it? Evolution itself is rejection in action. I don't give a damn if this book doesn't sell a single copy or that anyone who reads it thinks it's crap! There's no difference between success and failure, that's what Jock has shown me! That's the lesson I've learned! If you want some more modern art, you can't do better than this – a book written by a non-writer; a message in a bottle no one's going to read! I've made my point and I'm happy! It's not fame and wealth I want, it's communication, for someone to say, "Hey, that's right, I understand what you feel!" I want to reach people like me who feel that life is godless and not very meaningful and that their one small life is devoid of greatness, that whatever they do, some other bugger does it better; knows more than them and rubs their insignificance in their faces. John Cage chose silence to express nothing. I have chosen a rant and a tantrum! They'd publish this diary if I was a murderer, wouldn't they? Or some other rotten criminal, but I'm worthless because I haven't broken any major mores. I haven't caused some wild sensation in the world! I'm just a nobody! If I'd run amok with a gun then sold my story, that would make the difference, but running amok with a pen doesn't grab the attention so much does it! Well, you just wait, my friends! You just wait! I won't give away the plot but if you see me coming wielding an axe, don't hang about!

...I'm sorry, I lost it back there. It's the worry of the seminar. No excuses. I'm sorry. It was rude of me. It won't happen again.

The Seminar

Jock was on his third 'Special Brew' before he agreed to come with me. I managed to convince him that this was his one big chance to put two fingers up at the world that had repressed him. We were laughing like old friends on the way. He'd lost that suspicion and hostility towards me. I saw that I was as homeless as he was, detached, isolated, forgotten as he. His existence, his audacious existence crashed against the corridors of the department of philosophy. He didn't care. Nothing could turn awareness back on himself. He'd lost all self-consciousness. I supported him as he laughed and stumbled.

"Wait here until I get you," I said, "and try to keep quiet."

"OK," he whispered hoarsely. God! He stank!

The students gradually assembled through the far end of the lecture hall as I arranged my notes. Eventually, everyone was seated and I stood up. My nerves were jangling.

"In the first part of my talk, I am going to explore how various thinkers and various traditions have understood the 'self concept', concentrating mainly on the sociological, psychological, existential and Buddhist...."

A loud belch could be heard outside and there was a smattering of laughter. Hines, seated to the side of me, showed no emotion.

"In the second half, I want you to listen to my guest speaker."

Jock started singing and swearing. I cleared my throat.

"On second thoughts, perhaps we ought to have the guest speaker on first."

I went to help Jock in. He emerged, grinning, drunk. I directed him towards the rostrum where he held himself up.

"Over to you Jock," I said.

"Right.... Well...."

He stared out at the students. They were all grinning with disbelief and confusion. They wondered if it was a rag week joke. I couldn't remember seeing so much attention. Smiles wipe away pretentiousness; they were all on his side.

"My mate wants me to talk about my opinion on 'life'. Well... I'll tell you what I think... Well, I had a job, right? I had money, a missus and a fucking mortgage. I made a few mistakes and I lost the lot. Good job, I say! Good fucking job!"

I smiled nervously, wondering if this was such a good idea after all.

"You see," Jock continued, "You get a job and spend your whole life trying to buy a pile of bricks from a load of rich bastards who lend you the money, wanting ten times back what they lend you... These bastards are rich because they rip us off! They're like bloody drug pushers! Bastard mortgage pushers!"

There was some laughter and some mild applause. Jock continued.

"They've got it all worked out - I tell ya..." said Jock with a definite crescendo. "They know you've got to have a woman and if you've got a woman you're going to need somewhere to live, right.?... And they know you can't get anywhere to live without them ripping you off, and these are the same bastards that give you a fucking awful job so that you can pay them back all the money they force you into borrowing... I tell you, it's all crap! It's all a sham, all a swindle. I'm out of that! I don't owe no fucker nothing!"

Jock took a deep breath and surveyed his audience, grinning wickedly like a debauched king before his subjects. His voice dropped to a whisper as he leant forward and stared into the eyes of the front row.

"I watch all those suited, clean shaven and tidy men looking at their watches, hurrying to get to work as if the world couldn't fucking do without them!"

The length of the sentence had him gasping at the end. He'd misjudged it and hadn't taken enough air on board. He took a huge breath to compensate and his next few words bellowed out, rattling in the audiences' eardrums.

"Wankers! The lot of 'em! They've got fuck all, just the same as me, but they don't see it, see!"

A yellow finger jutted forward with such ferocity, people flinched, as if their eyes had been poked out. Some had stopped smiling but joined in as a small ovation began to ripple from a group of 'trendies'.

Steve was at the back, laughing quietly to himself and taking notes. He was writing something about an ethnomethodological experiment where common-sense situations are disrupted to see how social order was constructed. The 'meaning' of this odd event had been created and established as a 'joke'. The students were laughing with relief that chaos was not really happening. Hines didn't know what to do. His interpretation was different. Something resembling anger was on his face. I took hold of Jock's arm and tried to wind up his speech.

"Thank you, Jock," I said. "You have given us a good illustration of how the social, economic and central value system can alienate the individual and shape the self concept. There are people here who get paid huge salaries for writing about the stuff you know first hand. You know as much as any psychologist or sociologist."

I announced a short interval as I guided Jock outside again. I patted his back.

"Well done, Jock. Thanks. You were great," I said. I stuffed packets of cigarettes in his grubby coat.

"You didn't realise, you idiot! I was taking the piss. I took the piss out of you taking the piss out of me! I'm not even that pissed. I was acting. I got one over on you!"

"We're all acting, " I said. "All the time, it's the sociological concept of self that I've got to talk about now. Do you want to stay for it?"

"You must be joking. I'm off. Next time it's a crate, all right!"

"All right," I said.

Not altogether surprisingly, Hines 'wanted a word'. Funny how 'authority figures' still evoke a feeling of fear, no matter how enlightened you might be. Steve could explain this no doubt - a conditioned response.

"You like to be controversial," said Hines, his voice dangerously cold. "Your essay and your seminar seemed to rely on shock tactics. This is philosophy that we're involved in, not drama. Have you considered drama?" It sounded like a nice way of asking me to bugger off. I think he was still bitter about my discovery that he too was a human, he too masturbated, fantasising about beautiful young girls in a most unprofessional way...

"No, I haven't, " I said. "Drama is about fiction. I'm only interested in the truth."

"You're only interested in making a big impact, it seems to me," said Hines.

I resisted the temptation to say, "Yes Dad!"

Instead I told him that I was going to leave university. He was not one to show any emotions, but I assumed that this was not the worst news he had ever received in his life. I was going to take off, maybe abroad.

Later in the pub, Steve started getting heavy with me. I was flattered. It's nice to know that someone actually gives a shit about you. It'd be better, of course, if he was female and had all the right parts, but his heart was in the right place.

"I think you ought to finish your degree," he said. "You only want to give it up because it's important to you and you can't bear the thought of something being important. And you're not being honest with yourself. In fact, your obsession with authenticity is inauthentic; you're just using this idea to run away from the truth, and from yourself. You *have* to be a self; you cannot be a non-self, whatever you call it…. There's no getting away from the fact that you exist…."

"I don't exist," I protested, "I feel nothing. I believe in absolutely nothing!"

"That's not enlightenment; that's just being 'fucked up' in the head. You need treatment. You're not a mystic; you're a loony!"

"Thank you for your diagnosis," I said, smiling, "But aren't you being a fascist? If I reject the social values of my culture, aren't you using psychiatric diagnosis as a political weapon?"

With his usual literary device, Steve rolled a cigarette to break up the dialogue. He shook his head with fatherly disapproval. I sometimes wondered if Steve was a father figure to me, but that's more psychobabble crap.

"So, what's hiding behind this academic language that you're using, if not a 'self' -a self that's trying to survive and protect itself? A no self doesn't use sarcasm does it?"

"A no self uses sarcasm when the situation arises to use it. A no self enjoys sarcasm as one of life's many blessings. Sometimes, sarcasm is appropriate, sometimes laughter, sometimes screaming, sometimes dancing, sex, stupidity. The moment dictates the mood."

"Moods are aspects of personality, not moments," said Steve. Did he have to defend his academic discipline every hour of the day? Couldn't he just be 'himself' – i.e. nothing? - Just a free spirit staring into the incomprehensible. He's trying to make something of himself- knew I shouldn't have trusted the earring!

"Personality is an illusion. Reality is an illusion. It's a house of cards – logic, words, ideas. Existence is beyond all this…."

Steve shook his head. He thought I was bullshitting again.

"You've got a son and you can't face the reality of it, so you run away, pretending you've no self and no responsibility. You're playing a game with yourself that you don't quite believe. You'll have to face it if you really want to be authentic. Face the shit that really exists!"

I prostrated myself upon the floor.

"Thank you, Master!" I said. I had an audience and Steve looked shocked and horrified.

"Get up!" he muttered.

"Am I embarrassing you?"

"Just a little," Steve muttered again.

I sat back down on the chair. Eventually, the heads stopped turning and the laughter subsided.

"Fatherhood might give your life structure. We all need our roles. No matter what you say, we need a 'backbone'."

"But I don't need nappies, sleepless nights...all that shit." I said, aware that I was only playing out the standard male script.

"Why? Life is shit anyway so you keep telling me, so what's wrong with really getting your hands in it. You're just afraid."

"I'd like to see him... I think," I said.

"You don't have to marry her. You just have to buy him birthday presents and take him to the park."

"And pay out money I haven't got. She's blackmailing me. This is unbelievable. Remember when I said life was like a bad story? If this was a story, the author's just trying to prolong my life. Just to pad it out a bit. He's got no more ideas!"

"Look...there's no story," said Steve. "You got her pregnant. It's actually what sex is ultimately about... She'd had your baby. You can't just pretend it didn't happen."

I sipped my pint thoughtfully. What Steve said was right in many ways, and I'd known this for a while.

"I suppose I had better surrender myself to the authorities," I said.

"And surrender to the real – the empirical."

Thursday

I went to see my son. He sat quietly in the middle of a chaos of toys and plastic bricks.

"He's not always this quiet, you know," said Anny.

It was a shock to see her. She had put on so much weight. Her hair was pulled back past her ears. She had no make-up. She was wearing an old sweatshirt and leggings. There was no shape discernible beneath them. I wanted to turn and run.

"I've got no money," I said, looking into the frightened child's face.

"Graduates get jobs"

"Not philosophy graduates."

"I'm sure they do. I'm prepared to wait, to be reasonable."

"I had the test done yesterday."

"There was no-one else..."

"I had to have it done."

"Would you like a cup of tea?"

I felt like laughing. It seemed so inappropriate, but I accepted. We sat and talked practicalities. I felt like I had been sucked back into the past. I could see her gradually taking control, as she had always done. An old forgotten hostility returned like a virus in the bones of a long dead skeleton. I started to feel nauseous.

"Can I have a glass of water?" I said. I just wanted to stop her talking.

"You look terrible," she said, unsympathetically.

"It's a shock. I feel a bit sick."

"The toilet is on the left if you need it."

"I won't."

Anny called Matthew to her, but he wouldn't come. He continued to sit there, eyeing me with great suspicion.

"Come on Matthew. This is your Daddy!"

"He obviously hasn't heard all good about me," I said.

"That's hardly surprising, is it?"

"There are two sides to every story," I said.

Matthew pushed a car along the floor, amongst the bricks and I found myself wanting to know him, pick him up, do things that 'dads' do. Here was the innocent, egoless human existence in all its purity, and I had created it - half of it, anyway. I felt a great dislike for Anny, for depriving me of his first years. I'll never see him as a baby. I asked for photographs. She had some. Her hideous old dragon of a mother couldn't even bring herself to smile in these shots. She was hating and condemning me in every one. They say to look at the mother if you want to see what your girlfriend will look like in years to come. Already she was becoming her, their genes pulling together with each year. Their reality was about tidy rooms, clean glasses, controlling people, judging people, being 'better' than other people in their small social circle. An illegitimate child was an inexcusable horror to her mother. A small piece of gold around a finger and some mumbo jumbo would have made the whole thing respectable.

"I don't get any money from them anymore. Daddy's business went bust a year ago."

She still said "Daddy" and "Mummy" like a silly schoolgirl. I hated it then, like I was hating it now, and hating myself for hating.

"I don't think..." I began, "I don't think that a marriage would work."

Anny threw back her head and laughed horribly – a slightly upper class bark and snort. I felt like strangling her.

"I want financial maintenance, nothing more. This is your child and you must share the burden."

"I have my rights too. If I'm going to give you money, I must have rights of access."

Anny pushed a strand of hair back over her ear. It looked like horse hair. Her horse-like nose snorted with disapproval.

"That's something for the authorities to sort out," she said.

A question mark formed itself in my mind and grew so big that I just had to ask her.

"What happened? I mean, I thought you were on the pill, weren't you?"

She had apparently stopped taking it when we were splitting up. Matthew was conceived in one of our 'hate sex' sessions. It was sad that he didn't even qualify as a 'love child'. What a start in life! To be composed of my genes and hers seemed to be bordering on cruelty! Yet I went back, feeling strangely elated, as if a real adventure had happened, as if there had been an interesting change of scenery. I had taken part in the human race. He would have a future, stretching out before him and I had set it in motion. I had created life. It was an amazing thought!

Friday

I went to see Hines again. I went to crawl to him and to apologise. He was not impressed.

"I understood that you were leaving the university," he said coldly.

"I need to finish it now. Things have changed. Something 'real' has happened in my life. I have to become.... *responsible*. I want to get a degree and a 'good job' afterwards. I have a renewed enthusiasm. I have the glimmerings of a real 'identity'"

"Seminars are not stand up comedies," said Hines.

"It wasn't a comedy. He had a perfectly valid view. He was the voice of the oppressed. He had an intuitive Marxist perspective. He...."

"It was conducted with an air of mockery and received as such."

"What if I apologise?" I said.

"The faculty has already been informed of your leaving. No doubt they have contacted the borough that deals with your grant."

"Could they not be informed that I've changed my mind?"

Hines said that I would have to go and sort it out myself and not to expect any support from him. This was just childishness played by adults. I'd spoilt his serious game and he was retaliating. I went to sort out the problem with the faculty. Administration is like a run-away juggernaut with no one in it. Once something is set in motion, it has its own momentum and nobody can stop it-a human creation, an impotent Frankenstein's monster that blunders onwards doing nothing of relevance.

"I'll have to go out to work then," I heard myself say. Called up to die for my country at last!

Steve and I had a celebratory drink and spliff in the union bar. We had both matured in recent months and reached certain milestones befitting of our ages! Steve was going to work hard and reach his goal, spurned on by the support of his new girlfriend. I was going out into the real world to support my child. I never could take philosophy seriously and I was beginning to wonder whether all that stuff in the park was just a bit of a 'breakdown', rather than an insight into existence itself. The world seemed more solid when you felt compelled to do something. I don't feel 'free' anymore but it's no loss. Who wants to be free and who wants 'truth'? - Only people with nothing to do.

"What are you going to do?" said Steve.

"I haven't thought about it, but there's one thing I've always dreamt about...."

You've guessed it, - Steve rolled a cigarette and tongued the shiny strip with the expertise of a French lover.

"Tell me your dreams?" said Steve, with irony in his eyes.

"Well, I've always wanted to be a writer. In fact, I've been writing a diary ever since I arrived, before I even unpacked. It's what all existentialist fictitious characters do. It's what Sartre's hero had to do to save his soul and to look back upon his life 'without repugnance'. It's what I want to do too. I think it would 'save me', even if it was just to cock a snook."

"I wish I could help," said Steve, puffing smoke, "And I'd like to read it." I didn't know whether or not he truly meant it.

"You can read it if it ever gets published," I said, "but I doubt that it ever could be. I know I'm not a *real* writer but I have to keep going with it. I reckon my tale expresses the frustrations of many people and I have to get this anger and confusion out of my system and connect with people I don't even know."

"So you're no longer a 'no self' then?" asked Steve. "No selves don't strive."

I finished my fourth pint.

"I've had some insight into my ego and into existence, but I'm not ready for the full disappearance yet. I'm not ready to live 'without a head' as D E Harding wrote about. I've still got some way to go yet."

"So who's winning? Buddha or Sartre?" laughed Steve apparently confused. I shrugged my shoulders.

"Who cares?" I said, and held out my empty glass.

* * *

Today my life comes to an end. Alone, free like the dead. The blood test confirmed that Matthew was not mine after all. Anny was as shocked as me. I yelled at her over the telephone. The queue of students behind me was listening with relish.

"What are you getting so upset about? You're off the hook now!"

"You said there was no-one else!"

"There wasn't. Except for a brief...."

"You said there was no-one else!"

"I'd forgotten. I didn't even know his name. I'll never track him down."

"You don't know what you've done to me, you evil bitch!"

"What are you talking about? Why aren't you out celebrating?"

I kept swearing at her until the phone went dead. I walked out into a warm setting sun and smiled. How sweet the feeling; indifference, emptiness. Non-existence, no self was my refuge. I had to become 'pure'; a pure existing non-thinking being that expected nothing, nothing at all. No striving, no hoping, no trying, no regretting, no past, no future. I'll exist like a puddle that forms on the pavement as you're pissing up a wall. This is existential despair. This is liberation!

I stared at the ceiling for hours, wondering what to do and where to go. I had hardly any money, I'd lost my place at university and the prospect of love was receding faster than my hairline. I remembered a line from one of Camus' books. It was about suicide being the only true philosophical question. Is life really worth living? Laugh a minute, old Camus! But he had a point. Suicide is the ultimate expression of human free will, isn't it? The genes would frantically put across their point of view, appealing to Darwinism and Ethology, insisting that I was biologically programmed to survive, and yet I could defy all that and go against my very basic nature. The idea fascinated me!

"What utter crap! " I hear in my head. An elected spokesman from the DNA society, "What kind of free will does a corpse have, eh? "

"The free will not to go on suffering pointlessly. That was what Camus was saying."

"Camus was a wanker, then! Don't be such an idiot! Can you imagine what an amazing gift life is? Can you imagine the incredible odds that make you what you are? "

"Don't take me to be such a fool. This is your own self-interest. Yes, I have read Richard Dawkins as a matter of fact, and I know your selfish nature. You just want another crack at creating another human. That's all that matters to you. I don't count for anything. You care nothing for consciousness. You don't care how I feel. You're just a load of bloody robots, only after one thing. Well, look! You've failed, and I've failed you. You should have planned this more carefully and I would have cooperated more. You should have given me a strong, handsome body and a face women can't resist, and a dynamic personality, then I'd do all the work you want. I promise you, I'd impregnate and run. You can't expect me to do the work without the correct tools! "

"There's still time. You're not even thirty years old yet. When you get older, there will be younger women who look for maturity...Look, can't we talk this through? You're misunderstanding something here. Biology is everything, including culture, including your experience of free will.

Consciousness is biology too. It has a biological function.....Don't you see?"

"You're getting desperate. I'm not listening. All I know is a feeling of intolerable suffering that I have the power to stop."

"Life is suffering, yes. And competitive and dangerous but there is a way out of it. Listen to the Buddhists"

I laughed.

"You are desperate! Using religion to save your skins! Leave Buddhism out of this. It's got nothing to do with you."

"Is your suffering comparable to the sort of suffering that goes on in the world? The wars, the famines, the disasters and bereavements?"

"An odd logic! Because others have it worse, I should be happy. That's a crap ethic! "

"It's called gratitude! You self centred little shit! Try relieving other people's suffering, then you're own might not seem so bad! "

"'Psychological egoism' - I help others to make myself feel better. That's inauthentic. That's clutching at straws. That's using people for my own ends."

"It makes for a better world! It makes a society possible! You don't know what it's like to share!"

"That's because no one will give me the bloody chance! "

"That's because you're not looking for sharing; you're just looking for 'shagging'!"

"And whose fault is that?"

Silence! I had them stumped. They'd dug their own hole and fallen into it. I was pleased with myself. I'd out argued my gametes. I'd won the dual, but for the final shot.

I left my books where they were, gathered up my money and walked out into the May sunshine. I bought six cans of 'Special Brew'- enough for a coma, and headed for the park. I walked across the road when 'the man' was red. Cars screeched, voices cursed. I laughed.

"Do you want to get yourself killed! " someone yelled, waving a fist.

"Yes!" I replied. 'Ethnomethodology' again! Such a question is never answered in the affirmative and so had to be interpreted as sarcasm, absolute impertinence. What would happen now? The driver had been insulted and taunted, unprovoked. This was an aggressive challenge, yet other variables were at work. He was on his way to work, stopping would hold up the traffic; violence would be seen by witnesses; his aggressive impulse may be overridden by cognition of the consequences. He may even not be bothered.

"Wanker!" the driver yelled and gave me a simulated demonstration of the said act. (He did not impart any new information.) He drove off, wishing he'd knocked me down.

I went into the Chemist and picked up some Paracetamol - a large pack, and put it into my pocket. I went into the park and sat down on the bench, looking at the same tree that had given that brief flash of enlightenment, now a distant memory.

The Paracetamol nestled in my hand like a grenade. Like my genes, it had a voice too. Hearing voices is a symptom of schizophrenia, but it's too late for that now. "Come on then..." it whispered in a pharmaceutical sort of way. Always seems that the triumphs of technology are put to improper uses - nuclear bombs, germ warfare, drug dealing. All had noble origins, and now I was about to use headache relief to answer Camus' question. I'm not really sad, either. I'm just doing a pointless act to stop a pointless existence. Does that sound self-pitying? I think it does a bit. If I'm going to do it, it has to be authentic. I'm not going to kill myself on some emotional whim. It has to be done with integrity and commitment or not at all.

I took out the packet and looked at it. It was as attractive as a birthday present. It could have contained a toy within it. I burped, feeling a gentle wave of alcohol break over me, the world becoming more easily absorbed, softer around the edges, giving me something to float in. I opened the second can....

The paracetamols were in blister packs. I listened to them crinkle and crack in the plastic - like a child with those sheets of packing stuff with air pockets they like to pop. They were a nice shape too, within their plastic protection. Row upon row of efficient little soldiers in perfect formation, well turned out, ready for action, waiting for 'the off' - a triumph of technology and discipline.

The waves of alcohol became a little choppy, but I waded out, feeling the coolness rise up my legs and freezing my balls. I can tolerate the terrible horniness of women when it gets this far. This is usually where Plato takes precedence over pussy. I finished the second can. This was going to take all my courage...

What came into my mind was sympathy - a compassion for myself! It was bizarre. (I'll have to write to Carlsberg about this). I thought about the build up of poison and the sad, futile attempts to shake it off. Those kind hearted organs and systems that give me a life, each one an altruist, doing their best, devoted to my survival. It felt like I had no right; that my body wasn't really mine to kill!

I couldn't go through with it! I couldn't contemplate 'murder', because that's what it felt like. Not suicide, but murder- like killing bunny rabbits. The red light was on and I slammed on the brakes. No last minute intervention from Jesus Christ, just the thought of bunny rabbits.

I opened all the paracetemols and flicked them into the air, one by one, watching them soar like golf balls into the rough, never to be found. I opened my third can, but then fell asleep.

What woke me up was a huge shadow of the Grim Reaper, but he had Jock's gravel-like voice.

"What a state! " he said, "You look like shit, mate! "

I struggled to sit up and was hit by a wave of nausea- nothing existential about this one. It was due to three Special Brews. Jock looked at me. He pointed a yellow finger.

"There's three of those left," he pointed out, " Are they going begging?"

"Help yourshelf..."

Jock sat down and snapped open a can with a sigh.

"Nice afternoon," he pointed out.

"Yes. I've just been trying to kill myself."

"Nice afternoon for it."

"Didn't you hear what I said? "

"Yes. Didn't you hear what *I* said?"

"Yes, but it didn't seem appropriate."

"It's your life. It's your death," said Jock with a shrug, " Will you be wanting those other two, then?"

"Well, I thought I might try to kill myself later on. I might need something to wash a lethal poison down with."

"Seems a shame to waste them."

Jock helped himself. I didn't protest. He just couldn't care less about anything.

"You've sussed it, Jock. You've got it right. Indifference. It's the answer."

Jock hadn't heard.

"Come on, son. Let's get some soup. The sally army is just round the block..." he said, pulling me up.

But there was more than indifference now. There was compassion too.

Some Years Later

Like a finished, guttering candle, a sense of self still flickers in the shadows. Every day I wake up and find pictures at the back of my eyes. I never asked to go to the cinema but I've sat here for more than thirty years now, drooling popcorn, trying to follow a plot.

If there's a plot at all, it's reached the point where I'm unemployed and skint. I live in a bed-sit, funded by a certain local authority. Jock used to come around, but he doesn't anymore. He freaked at the thought of a 'housing habit' - a 'slippery slope' he called it. He warned me it would lead to 'harder things', like work, a wife, responsibility and mortgage repayments.

"Look Jock, " I appealed to him, " It's only a council flat! Not very different from a park bench or a railway arch. I can handle it!"

He shook his head with experienced disapproval, warning me of mobile phones and fax machines to come. I haven't seen him for months.

The dream of signing on with a degree was not to be. I was asked why I hadn't finished my course. The girl behind the desk had nine GCSE's and shapely breasts with her name attached to one of them.

"I had a few crises, " I said to a breast, " but I still managed to reach significant insights into the nature of existence - a useful management skill, I feel. "

"What sort of work do you want?" she said, the joke being brushed aside with intolerant eyelashes - an intolerance that seemed out of place with her young years.

I didn't understand her question. I don't *want* any kind of work. Why should I want to work? I'm not scared of work, only the alien values that go with it - the unreality of becoming one with it, putting in extra time, extra effort to 'get on', achieve, look busy, to be what you do. It's not a question of just doing something and getting paid for it. There you are in the staff directory - that's you! Your grade, your rank, your position in the hierarchy is defined for you and that's all you are. You have to accept their values, their norms, their codes of speech and conduct, their sense of seriousness.

Those breasts were inches from me. How could I be expected to think of a career and a future with breasts like that in front of me? Nothing ventured, nothing gained, I suppose...! Here goes!

"Will you come out for a drink with me?" I boldly ventured. Not a glimmer! Not a moment of surprise or hesitation or being caught off guard.

She was a real pro! Trained as efficiently as a soldier, she was in control, on her way up, fuelled by feminist independence and power, her warm body packed in ice, to be thawed at her convenience, for the male of her choosing.

"We are here to discuss your employment situation, " she pointed out.

"Yes, I know but I'm more interested in you at the moment, " I said, romantically.

She sighed and gathered up her papers. She muttered something about sexual harassment and left. A man shortly filled her place. He was not amused and urged me not to harass his staff. I protested, pointing out that if asking a young lady out constituted harassment, then we were all condemned to a life of loneliness and the human race would cease and...

"Look! This is irrelevant!" he barked at me. "I want you to look at some of these vacancies. Any more stupidity and I'll recommend that your benefit is stopped."

I looked at the vacancies and even followed some of them up. Within a vast ocean of barely changing emptiness, I pulled pints, plucked poultry and replenished shelves with tins like a nocturnal mammal in a faceless capitalist world. I revelled in the glorious feeling of being a victim. Victims have the strongest identities. Marx should have said: "Workers of the world unite! You have nothing to lose except that feeling of purpose when it's all over and there's nothing to fight for."

So here I am again, a new beginning in an old place, a feeling of 'deja vu'.

I had to prove each week that I was 'actively seeking work'. I had to keep a record of all the applications I had made. I'd apply for jobs and then give 'honest interviews'. The benefit office insists on honesty, but they don't like it so much when we're seeking work, but I found it great fun!

"So, why do you want to work for the Department of Trade?"

"Well, I don't really. I'm not all that interested in the way the country is run at the moment, as I haven't got a girlfriend and sorting out my personal life takes priority. However, I need to earn money to improve my material existence and to afford beer, of course, so I thought I'd better apply for the job."

In a world where deceit is the norm, honesty and frankness have no place and get reinterpreted as impertinence. So many years just passed like this! The world shrunk to a radio and a chair. I sat here, listening to world news with detachment, counting how many years I had left to live. I wondered if it was logically impossible to fight against apathy.

Between the adverts for mobile phones and new cars, the world news was standard stuff. International crises as regular and as boring as a bowel movement. The IRA killed someone; peace talks broken down, more hostilities between warring ethnic factions. One Christian sect shot a few people from the opposing sect that believed in essentially the same thing, in protest over a right to march up and down a street banging a drum, dressed in orange! One man's religious and political struggle is another man's comedy sketch!

And I don't fit in anywhere. I remain surplus to requirements to natural selection, genetically extinct and lack of funds has even stopped my 'purchases', I'm sad to say. The beauty of women seems to correlate with decreasing self-esteem. When you feel like shit, breasts seem like the answer to everything! I switch on the TV and drool at 'Sabrina, The Teenage Witch', American crap sporting the paragon of female perfection, the Messiah swirling down the bog. The TV is now on the blink and I had to take up reading again. I read and re-read Sartre, Camus, Kierkegaard, Barbusse, Dostoyevsky, Nietzsche...On a Saturday night too! I'm jealous of their talent and recognition and wish I could be as negative as they were.

Who knows of my existence? What have I done, what have I got that would warrant recognition? Nothing! I've done nothing, and I've seen that there's nothing to do or say or find or achieve! I've seen this! I've seen the deep yawning heart of indifference, and I'd like to share it with you, my imaginary friends! Like the glinting twisting blade, like the smoking gun turned inwards, a brief dance of the clown before the more important business. Achieving nothing is my purpose, my aim, my art! I have nothing to say! And I'll make you listen! I'll make you hear me out! I'll declare it from the roof- tops one day!

Eventually, I was sent to see a Psychotherapist. My GP, like a Soviet doctor, decided that my lack of interest in the working world or the political system was a 'symptom' of mental illness. My anarchic, 'fuck the system' standpoint was not considered genuine politics. I was 'mad' because I voted differently and consequently I was obliged to see the 'Status Quo doctor'.

In a surprise twist of fate, I have found that my therapist was none other than my lost friend, Steve. I know it's hard to believe!

"I don't believe it!" I said, grinning.

"I don't believe it!" said Steve. Neither of us could believe it. Steve seemed reluctant to shake my hand. You just don't shake hands with 'patients' or 'clients' or whatever else I'm known as. In helping others, Steve had to remember to be distant from them. I sat down in a rather nice, reclinable chair and looked around.

"Well, " I said, " You've done all right!"

"I got what I worked for, " he said. It sounded slightly smug to me.

"And what about that girl... Rachel?"

"Married her."

"I thought you might have done. Does she still dance? "

"No. She shops..."

I laughed and sighed with nostalgia.

"Hey! Isn't this great! " I said with delight.

Steve looked at me, signs of role conflict showing in his face and posture. He looked like a policeman, not knowing whether to arrest his best friend or turn a blind eye to a bank robbery. He flicked through the notes on his desk.

"The name from your GP seemed to be familiar but I didn't imagine that... I mean, I see a lot of people. "

I reclined in the chair with a sigh of satisfaction, looking up at the ceiling.

"What do you think? Manic depression? Schizophrenia? Multiple personality?"

I was like someone planning his holiday. Steve scratched his eyebrows; an interesting change in literary device.

"Given up the roll-ups, then? " I said.

"Long time ago, " he muttered. Something seemed to be bothering him.

"And the 'wacky backy'?"

Steve visibly flinched. He leant across his desk and whispered at me. He was 'respectable' now and he would thoroughly deny any leak of what he used to get up to. Nobody would believe me anyway and it would just be put down to my symptoms of mental illness. Poor Steve; he was clearly paranoid, but I just laughed, to make him feel better.

"That's an abuse of power, doctor," I said.

"I'm not a doctor, I'm a psychotherapist," he said with pride.

"So cure me, Mr Psychotherapist. Cure me of my angst."

No more wise grin. He now had a professional, functional smile, designed to put people at their ease. But it unnerved me. Here was a robot with self- esteem and a determination to protect it. He was dangerous.

"I can help you," he said, "if you cooperate and really want to change."

"Change?" I said, "What do you want to turn me into?"

"Change your outlook. You are carrying a lot of baggage. I can see it now like I saw it at college. You are very bitter about life. You are avoiding living because you are scared of the risks."

"What! No Schizophrenia? I'm disappointed."

"I'll not rise to your bait, Antoine. If you want to get better, you'll have to cooperate."

"Better? Better than what?"

"Better for yourself - more 'functional'."

"Functional for society?"

"That's a reasonable expectation. The world doesn't owe you a living."

"Patching up the wounded so that you can send them back to the frontline. I know what this is all about. Well Steve, I don't owe the world anything either. I don't want to work, for conscientious, philosophical reasons. It would be inauthentic. Shoot me if you must."

Steve scratched his eyebrows. (I really wish he hadn't given up smoking, the roll ups had so much more imagery, don't you think?)

"Malingering isn't a mental illness," he said.

"What about 'pathological' malingering? " I suggested, hopefully.

Steve shook his head.

"I'll have to fake the symptoms then. I know exactly how a Schizophrenic behaves."

"I'll catch you out," Steve promised.

A silence fell between us. I wish I knew why I felt this hostility towards him. I wish he could tell me. Perhaps I felt betrayed, jealous, inferior, superior? It was the 'identity' he had created for himself. He was inauthentic. Eventually, Steve spoke.

"What happened to you, anyway? You just disappeared. You left all your books."

"I learned something. I learned that learning is futile..."

Steve shook his head, almost imperceptibly and made some notes in my file.

"That diary thing you wrote at college; I want to read it," he said. I was surprised he had remembered. I had forgotten about it myself. It was confined to a bottom drawer after accumulating a trunk full of rejection slips. 'Thank you for your life which we regret is not suitable for our lists. We wish you luck in placing it elsewhere....'

"Why?" I asked.

"I think it may contain valuable data - about you."

I felt important. Steve was doing a good job already! I booked in another appointment and delivered the manuscript the next morning, before signing on. When I saw him again, I was full of anticipation, as if his opinion, or anyone else's for that matter, was the decisive factor. If he said it was crap, it was crap. If he said it was brilliant, that's what it was.

"It strikes me," said Steve, " that this diary comes directly from your unconscious mind. Each character, each episode has symbolic significance," he said at our next meeting.

"That sounds heavy," I said, with irony, but egotistically wanting more.

"I think 'Steve' is an aspect of yourself, for example. He isn't really me at all. A lot of these things in the book never actually happened, did they? I don't drink to excess, as 'Steve' does in the book. We never had many of these conversations that you invented."

"I call that 'denial', doctor."

"I told you, I'm not a doctor."

"Okay, I exaggerated a bit! A bit of 'poetic license' but of course you're you in my diary. If you're not you, who on earth are you?"

Steve asked me to relax. He jotted down some notes then came around from the other side of the desk. He spoke in a slow, measured, unreal way. It was difficult to suppress a laugh.

"I'm that part of you that struggles to come forward. You want to face reality, but you want to cling to your myths too. You can't bear the world to be an ordered place, where people get what they work for, if they've got the brains and talent. You want to reject my influence, but I cannot be pushed aside. There I am, alive in your unconscious mind, influencing you, fighting the irrational fool you set me against..."

"Irrational fool? Is that how you describe all your patients?"

"I'm only talking about an aspect of you. The 'fool' is that part of you that's stuck in the negative. The 'positive' is there, ready and waiting for you to act upon his good advice."

"You! The positive?"

"Yes, your internalisation of me into your unconscious. You'd like to be like me really, but you dare not. You dare not be anything, so you remain in purgatory, neither this nor that, stuck on the fence, incapable of jumping in any direction."

I laughed at him.

I saw Steve a few times more, but we were getting nowhere fast. He eventually wrote to my GP, telling him that I was not yet fit for work - a nice gesture of friendship, I thought. He recommended that I see a Psychiatrist. In the meantime, I was asked to swallow some psychotropic chemicals to help rectify a lack of morale among the shareholders of a huge pharmaceutical company. Naturally, I agreed, for a limited time period.

The psychiatrist listened intently to what I had to say, but I couldn't help but notice a flicker of boredom when I discussed, in great length, my sense of boredom. I still believed in nothing, I still negated everything everyone else believed in, I still felt that all opinions and goals were fake, just something to fill the gap between birth and death. I told him that all I wanted to do was write a book, to show to the world how clever I am.

"I've written several books," said Lloyd (his name) "and believe me, it's not as exciting as you might think."

Lloyd had a beard - a wispy, goatee, clichéd type thing. He wore a monocle, smoked a pipe and had an Austrian accent. Not really! But he did have a slightly balding head. Yawn...waistcoat, pinstriped trousers, black shoes, wart on his chin (no, forget that...!) aged about...ooh, I'd say fifty-five, maybe sixty, but he looked nothing like Hines - you remember him? Lloyd was much more robust, with a slight beer gut. He had a sort of 'academic refugee' look about him, as if all his books were burned over there in his native land, but were gaining acceptance here in the UK, Okay?

"Now, I want you to go back to that incident with the tree, where all boundaries seemed to melt..." said Lloyd at the start of one of our sessions.

"I've told you before, there was no incident. I just took Sartre's novel *Nausea* and took the mick out of it. "

"I hear what you say," said Lloyd, "But how your unconscious communicates is what interests me. Your last therapist suggested that there was essentially a conflict between the rational and non-rational within your personal constructs, and that a suitable resolution was to allow the rational to defeat the non-rational. However, I feel that this hypothesis should be reversed."

"Keep talking. We've got a lot of pages to get through..."

He looked at me with brief incomprehension and then filled his pipe.

Soon the air was filled with sweet smelling carcinogen.

"How do you propose that we get 'Steve' to accept your intuitive understanding of human existence? When I say 'Steve', of course, what I mean is your father. Through 'Reaction-formation', you have turned your father into a young man, someone of your own age, in fact. By levelling the playing field, you feel that a fairer contest is possible between you."

"Hey, this is *my* neurosis. Don't I get a say?"

Lloyd shook his head. It wasn't a neurosis; it was a 'spiritual crisis'. He went on to explain his own crises and how he had solved them through a mixture of Jungian psychology and some potent illegal substances, used exclusively for research into human consciousness and not just for 'fun'. I got the impression that he only felt it morally wrong if you enjoyed it - as all good Catholics know.

"How would you like to be a part of my work?" he asked, hopefully.

"Just to get over my writing block, the controlled use of illegal substances sounds very inspiring." I said with a nod. He was pleased and polished his monocle with enthusiasm.

June? August? It's all arbitrary...

"Sometimes we need to give the boundaries a little push," said Lloyd as he attached electrodes to my head. It was a warm evening and Lloyd had just given me a tour of his palatial home. He had obviously sold an awful lot of books and was fully intent on putting me into his next one. I thought there might be something in it for me too -anything to get me out of the council flat.

I swallowed the potion and lay back, waiting for it to kick in. The urge to giggle was my first reaction. Lloyd's serious note taking and observation of my brain waves seemed to be particularly amusing and absurd. The giggling didn't last long and I enjoyed a protracted period of peaceful calm, where everything seemed to have stopped, including time. I didn't expect or hope for anything else, but then it started to happen.

There, in front of me, a storm seemed to be brewing - like a 'twister'. I watched it gradually coming towards me. I began to feel a slight concern and told Lloyd about it. He asked me to describe it. It was just a gaping black hole, coming to claim me. I could just about hear Lloyd above my pounding heart.

"It sounds like a birth experience," he said. "Don't be afraid. It is only a birth canal."

"I prefer to see them from the other side," I said, "And not my mother's!"

Lloyd didn't laugh. My sense of humour also escaped me, as the 'twister' got nearer. I began to be drawn into it and started passing along a long, dark tunnel. At the end of the tunnel was a light that I had to reach. I remember thinking that perhaps I was dying and that it didn't really matter. On the way towards the light, a number of faces began to appear before me - a school teacher that humiliated me, a friend that betrayed me, a succession of rude and self important secretaries, an obnoxious boss, unfeeling colleagues, affluent mouthy women drivers in unnecessarily large safari-type vehicles, wearing dark glasses and chatting on mobile phones, hooting you up on the road, exasperated because you've hesitated for a micro-second - (I'd like to smack their arses!); faces of girls who had rejected me. They all looked at me, waiting for me to say something. I said a lot of somethings too. I swore at them, put two fingers up at them, attacked them with devastating sarcasm that had them recoiling. The words just flowed through me with a fantastic energy. I watched them dissolve or explode. I felt like my constipated psyche had finally pushed through some very stubborn emotional poo and I was at last free from their demonic influence.

I was just beginning to recover from this experience when I noticed that the tunnel had disappeared. I was lying on my back, looking up at a beautiful sun. My surroundings were like a prehistoric forest. I only hoped that I hadn't stumbled upon some rejected Sci-Fi plot, and half expected some Tarzan-like alien with an American accent to appear and talk about Elves and stuff. Mercifully, this didn't happen. It occurred to me that I was in 'paradise', and one huge improvement on my council flat and environs. This conclusion became more and more valid as I noticed the abundance of fruits on the trees, the warm lakes with overhanging trees and the most incredible, semi-clad beautiful woman beckoning me from a clearing in the woods. I walked towards her in disbelief.

She offered me her hand. I took it and looked into her eyes. An energy began to pour into me from the cosmos. I hovered my lips inches above her abundant, moist mouth, savouring the moment before I kissed her with a passion that was both tender and violent at the same time. In the story of my life, such a love scene was way, way overdue!

Her body in my arms sent shock wave after shock wave through mine. Her hair fell over her naked shoulders, as I guided her gently towards the carpet of leaves beneath us. As we 'made love' (yes, I *can* be romantic!), I could hear birds singing, joyfully. They urged me on to find her deep refuge of unbearable happiness. It was so much more than 'porno'; it was a dissolving of boundaries; it was turning away from the cave wall to see the source of the light; it was the quintessential sexual, love experience that everyone only dreams of; it was.... it was....great! I had just made love to every woman in the world that exists, that once existed and who will exist, (apart from the ugly ones). She was the essence of all femininity in the universe - the goddess, Shakti. I couldn't wait to get back and tell Steve that I'd just had sex with a goddess. Not many blokes could claim such an achievement! It was an incredible experience, and it goes without saying, I was somewhat depressed to leave her behind.

Lloyd only looked up from his writings when I started to take off the electrodes.

"Not yet," he insisted. He was still taking readings, still putting his Jungian, archetypal mysterious psychobabble into the draft version of his new book. He was almost in a frenzy of writing, prizes, University chairs, recognition in his eyes.

"I must get down as much as possible, while it is still fresh. I have deduced the general outline, but you must fill in the details," he said.

I told him everything that 'happened', but even though the experience seemed real and significant, a 'simple' explanation inched its way forward, spreading the dull news that my insight into the higher realms of human consciousness may have been nothing more than a fucked up, drugged brain. In other words, it wasn't real! Lloyd was too involved and enthusiastic to take much notice of my scepticism. He understood how I could doubt the experience of others, but not my own. What other than experience could pass as reality? he reasoned. I was unconvinced. I didn't believe in hallucinations.

I felt a certain pity for my psychiatrist and embellished my experiences for him. Over the months, I displayed symptoms of mental stability that Lloyd wrote about extensively, pretending my whole understanding of life had changed. We shook hands and parted. I could accept neither the rational nor the irrational. I was completely stuck, negating both atheism and theism with equal animosity. The fence had adhered to my arse.

My unconscious had created a new character - Lloyd, the user of words and images to force reality into his sense of mystery and the need for significance. He now took on the fight with the empirical, materialistic 'Steve', my archetypal father who wanted to cut off my penis and dominate my intellect. My unconscious was beginning to get a little crowded. That's what unemployment does to you!

My spiritual search continued. I spent my benefit money, (and a little something Lloyd had given me for my trouble), on various 'therapies' that promised to liberate me from my torment. I was pounded, pulsed, massaged; I joined encounter groups for some psychodrama. I painted pictures in 'art therapy', danced and sang in 'music therapy' sessions, I explored my 'inner child' and 'reclaimed' same; I married myself, did affirmations, self talk, self write, hypnosis, flotation, aromatherapy, acupressure and acupuncture, Bach remedies, (better and more accurately known as Brandy), homeopathy, (pills with nothing in them, but at least they had no side effects), Kinesiology (What crap!), Reiki, Shiatsu, (I didn't know if he was trying to cure me or bugger me), colour therapy (I didn't have enough 'orange', apparently), spiritualism, shamanistic travel, paganism, witchcraft, absent healing (there was certainly an absence of healing!) I joined a group of Red Indians from Camden Town and worshipped the Goddess in Aylesbury. I tried to believe that crop circles weren't created by a bunch of pranksters and that 'the aliens' came down years ago and mated with humans, that UFO's exist and the governments of the world know it, that ghosts exist... I ended up totally exhausted - well, every part of me except my scepticism, which grew all the stronger. I had to face it. I was alone, and I couldn't lose this sense of self that felt that way. I resolved to give up trying to give myself up.

Fame, at last!

I was just watching an incredibly boring TV chat show when there was a knock at the door. I leapt to my feet with enthusiasm, hoping it would be a plot. I stood back in surprise (again!). It was Steve, holding a carrier bag. He shook my hand, vigorously.

"I've got something to tell you!" he said, "Your diary is going to be published!"

I couldn't take it in. I felt like a lottery winner. Steve took several cans of strong lager from the carrier bag and snapped one open in triumph. Apparently, he had been discussing my case with a literary agent at an academic meeting and my diary had come up in the conversation. The agent said he'd like to read it and within a few weeks, he had found a publisher. He thought it witty, intelligent, original, expressing universal anxieties that rarely get mentioned or even fully acknowledged. He felt that it would be a cult book of the new millennium. A sense of unreality came over me; fact and fiction were becoming blurred and confusing again.

I didn't know if Steve was telling the truth. I didn't even know now if Steve even existed. Was he just a character in my unconscious like he said he was?

"Come on! Get drunk! We've got something to celebrate!"

Had we slipped back into the past again? How come he was his old, college self again, instead of the successful psychotherapist? I waited all evening for an explanation. The only thing I could think of was that he wanted to be all chummy with me again because he thought there might be some money in it for him. We got drunk, like old times. I wondered how I could maximise sales of my diary. The usual strategy was either crime or insanity, or both. I thought about murder. Who could I kill? If all values are relative then it made sense to use any means to promote my book. It was an interesting thought.

"I reckon lots of the nutters that run amok and massacre innocent people have got something to say, but they know no one's going to listen," I said.

"What?" said Steve, taken off his guard.

"They're basically all tongued- tied and mind- tied. They try to say what's going on inside them but all the words just come out as bullets."

"That's cool," said Steve with a belch and a smile. He assumed I was joking.

"I know it sounds funny, but I've always felt an empathy for the gun-toting psychopath on the rampage. He's basically misunderstood. I've often thought that this could be my destiny."

"You're just trying to be shocking," said Steve. He started rolling a cigarette.

"When did you take that up again?" I asked, beginning to suspect that something very odd was going on. Steve was mellowing out, back on the scene, re-integrated, no longer the unconscious, archetypal castrating father figure.

"William James, in his *Varieties of Religious Experience* says that alcohol is a positive thing in human life. It makes us say 'yes' instead of 'no'" I said, changing the subject. "I've just been reading it. I agree with him. Knowledge through alcohol – e*pissed*temology! Sartre knew it and Jock sure as hell did! That's a great title for my book – The E*pissed*temologist. Tell them I want to change the title, Steve!"

"I will."

Two cans snapped and hissed in unison. The knowledge-giving substance was working its way to my brain and my mind was back on philosophical questions:

"Scientists have to reject the idea that we have free will," I pondered, "because everything has to have a cause."

"You never give up, do you?" Steve laughed.

" - A sense of self has to be an illusion too, since ultimately we are nothing but the firings of neurones."

"Yes, but it doesn't matter," said Steve. "Mind has its own reality - even if it doesn't really exist. We've had this before."

"But what's amazing is that Buddhists say the same thing. They too say that a sense of self is an illusion."

"Yes? So?"

"Well, doesn't it seem odd that science and 'mysticism' reach the same conclusions? I think I'm being drawn more and more towards Buddhism. They've definitely got something. They definitely *know* something. But I'm afraid to invest any hope in it. I so don't want to think it's crap!"

Confusion and enlightenment flicked on and off in my brain; like at a fairground, trapped on the ghost train, shocked by the laughing skeletons falling out of cupboards as I turned tight corners that led to more monsters. For several minutes, I sat with my head in my hands, like an executioner inspecting his work. A terrible feeling started to race within me -the down side of e*pissed*temology!

"We don't really exist at all," I blurted out, suddenly horrified. "We're just waves of probability; we exist or don't exist in other worlds too. Every time I come across a fork in the road, I split into two and take both forks in different dimensions.....and *time*...time runs backwards in other universes...

We die then get younger. We'll have to go to the doctor's when we're six and hear the bad news that soon, we won't be able to walk anymore, that we'll soon be in a cot and lose the power of our limbs and bowels. It'll be no different, except that we'll be wise first, then become the irritating student, then think we know it all, then play with toys, then, then then......"

"Take it easy! " Steve warned. "This is 'pressure of speech'. It sounds like you're going into a psychotic episode. Calm down. Try not to get excited! Hey! You're not putting this on, are you? "

"I'm malingering, malingering, malingering all my life, doctor- looking for an identity, like sand running through my fingers, never believed in anything, not sure I even believe in Darwin anymore, bears turning into whales, the idea that we evolved from bacteria is just as hard to believe as Noah's ark. Are there ever any spontaneous genetic mutations that could be beneficial and selected for by nature? The whole theory seems like just another story; just like Adam and Eve; just air from human lungs, words that are nothing but shapes formed by vocal cords, there is no reality to find, there are no answers, not even any questions!... I knew I was being lied to at school, at work; it was all false! All false, I tell you! I always knew! Always, always knew all along! Ha! Ha! They just wanted to control our minds, fill it with false things, false values, exams, careers, money, beliefs, all false! They wanted to keep the truth from us, that's there's no truth! I'm an observer from another planet, sent here to observe human behaviour, I can only observe, I tell you, I'm a mind that watches itself, that's how Camus described an intellectual, a mind that watches itself! I watch, I see the emptiness behind the façade; there's glass around me, unbreakable glass, people think it's flesh but it's glass, glass, glass! And when it finally shatters....when it finally shatters!...."

Steve looked at me with increasing concern and confusion. I was as good as a housewife faking an orgasm.

"The nutters that run amok," I continued to rant, "When they've committed evil, they know what they are. They have an identity. They are free - free from the self. They show us how ineffective the 'red light' really is; they plough on through, creating carnage and chaos like works of modern art. They become one with indifference, with senselessness, with inexplicable chance, inexplicable life...I know how they feel! I've brushed against their state of mind and I understand them! They see life as absurd and they want to destroy it! Get rid of what's absurd! Erase what is pointless!...Steve! Steve! I'm going to kill! Kill! Kill! Unless you stop me!

Help me! Stop me!"

Like a cowboy in a crappy western, Steve reached for his mobile phone. With great relief, I was eventually taken away to a psychiatric hospital where I continued to rant incoherently for several hours. I was considered a danger to myself and others and needed to be kept under observation, and drugged up to the eyeballs. Eventually, I fell into a strange calm, waiting for a psychiatric diagnosis that would turn my spiritual search into an aspect of pathology. They were quick to make a connection with my 'episode' and my use of LSD. Lloyd was tracked down and questioned but managed to display a career-saving loophole. He had a licence to use it.

In hospital, I felt a great sense of resolution and peace. I even felt 'happy'. My consciousness, my inner experience was spreading out into the collective unconscious, making connections to other minds - other pinched off and separated experiences of the universal intelligence. It felt like I had really done something, that I was at last, *something*. I was immortalised in print. It was also a good move to be in a mental institution from a sales point of view. People always buy books written by nutters. I remember a good piece of advice from an established writer. Never admit to being a husband with two children. That'll get you nowhere. Always be a convict, madman, spy or terrorist. That's what people want.

"They think you have both an inferiority complex and delusions of grandeur," said Steve one morning. I frowned with incomprehension, as I often do.

"That's possible, is it?"

"In the world of Psychiatry, yes. You'll going to be kept in for observation for a while, just until we're certain you're not dangerous."

"I'm in no hurry to return to my flat, " I said, " Not until there's something worth going out for."

"And what would that be?" said Steve.

"Recognition. For people to read and understand my diary."

Steve nodded. There was something on his face that I did not recognise.

Out, at last!

Drifting through space and time, I awoke and watched the world go in and out of focus. Steve was standing above me, looking uneasy, as far as I can still read and understand faces. I felt very odd and wondered if it was LSD revisited.

"What happened? " I asked the blurring faces. I heard Steve clear his throat.

"They erm... gave you some treatment, " he said. " ECT. I advised against it, myself."

I made a mental note that the next time I saw a couple of lunatics coming at Steve with an iron bar, I would advise them against it. Soon, it was only Steve that remained in the room with me. I felt almost too weak to speak, but I had to try.

"You'll have to tell them, " I said. " Tell them that you knew I was faking it."

Steve wrung his hands, but no sound came out. He also knitted his brows and was so anxious he could have made a winter hat. As you can see, ECT didn't destroy my sense of humour.

"But I didn't! " said Steve, " I didn't know you were faking it. I don't know now whether you're faking it or not, or whether you're mad and faking sanity! I hadn't anticipated this ...."

"You know what..." I whispered, a bit like 'Droopy', "Psychology is shit..."

Steve sighed. His eyes flickered with shame; his nose twitched with remorse.

"I'll get you out," he said with sudden inspiration, " Leave it to me!"

You'll forgive me if this diary seems a bit rambling and disjointed at the moment. I somehow doubt that Shakespeare's sonnets would be quite what they were if he had had his head wired up to the National Grid like I had. (I had wanted to feel more 'alive', not bloody *Live*.) A word of advice to the reader - never fake mental illness – you'd have to be mad to do so!

Eventually, Steve secured my release. He explained that I had been a 'pseudo-patient' in a replication of Rosenhan's work as a PhD thesis. Eventually, his story was accepted but he was booted out of his professional body. He was found guilty of transgressing the ethical code and of wasting the time of the psychiatric staff. They promised him that he would never work again. That was spirited of them! Sad to say, this took its toll on Steve. He took a turn for the worse, unable to cope with unemployment and unable to take the stress of a wife that couldn't take the stress of his unemployment, he started to get visibly down. Rachel saw him through this difficult period, at least until she realised that her credit cards were useless in the fashionable shops. Then, of course, she took off.

Steve pretended that he could cope and tried to give the impression that since the breakdown of relationships was part of everyday life, he knew how to deal with it. Despite his bravery, I could sense that he was adrift, his ordered and verifiable world cut loose from him. He was depressed and struggling against it. Trapped between his own feelings and his own self-image, he tortured himself.

"Steve," I said, "You're only depressed because you're attached to illusions; illusions of self, status, success...Give it up, Steve. Give up your mind."

"I've lost everything," Steve admitted, his head held briefly in his hands,

"Everything is nothing; nothing is everything. Form is emptiness and emptiness is form." I said, helpfully.

"I thought she loved me. She only loved coats, dresses and shoes."

"Steve, one thing I've learned when I was in hospital was that even depression is used as an attempt to escape freedom and anguish. It doesn't work. You can't define yourself as a 'depressive' because your depression is only a choice. Enjoy your depression; it's not very different from joy, is it? It's being consumed with emotion. Both are a pleasure. Both are transient and unreal."

Steve came to live with me, as he had no friends anymore. He seemed a little more cheerful as the weeks and months went by and the bin liners filled with empty beer cans. The old days had returned, the circle had spun around again.

"You know what?" mumbled Steve, one evening, "No, let me tell you something interesting....I went for a walk today, in the woods, and I felt different to everything that was there. I knew that the trees and the stream and the leaves had their place, but me walking amongst all this was somehow *alien*. My consciousness, my mind, amongst all this stuff was peculiar, odd, weird! I stood listening to the stream, but wondered if there really was any sound, except in my head. It was like being at the zoo, taking notes, not really part of what I was seeing...I'm just trying to tell you, it was the opposite to your experience... I felt *disconnected* - an intruder. I didn't feel any barriers dissolve. I felt the opposite, like I didn't belong to nature at all..."

I felt sorry for Steve. I'd never had believed that he could have got like this. His solid personality with a place in the world had dissolved somewhat.

He was losing his identity and looking for a new one. He was turning in on his inner experience instead of looking for rules that animate us.

"The feeling of separateness is an illusion," I said, wanting to believe my own words. Somehow, I had become more positive as Steve had become more negative. The poles had switched. I was negating his negativity, but I longed for the complete dissolution of oppositions. How I longed for fame, fortune and females. How I longed to be free from the desire for them! Swinging between caring and not caring, the pendulum swings, sweeping back and forth through worlds of sanity and insanity, fact and fiction, understatement and exaggeration. I cling to the pendulum, like Tarzan, proclaiming my existence with a shout of the absurd.

"Rachel wants a divorce," said Steve.

"This probably isn't the right time then to ask you why I've had no money – from my book, I mean."

Steve looked mournful. He tried to change the subject.

"You're not ripping me off are you? You're not taking all my royalties?" I said.

"It's worse than that, I'm afraid. I paid for its publication myself. I never met any literary agent. I wanted to make you happy. You were always saying that you had to find out what was more important – happiness or the truth. You were falling into nilhilism and I wanted you to see that happiness can be better, even if it was only for a while"

"My diary..." I gasped, as if a child had been mortally injured.

"There's still a chance that people will read it. It's just that it's not... mainstream."

He could not disguise what he really thought, despite his best effort. He didn't think it was good enough to be 'mainstream'. He must have seen the pain in my eyes as my happiness shrivelled into truth. He tried to comfort me and justify himself.

"Publishers are so stuck in their ways. They only think about sales and money. Your diary is authentic; it's *real*. That's why I published it. That's why I'm skint!"

"I was an *experiment*! I was your bloody *monkey*!" I gasped.

"No, it wasn't like that! It was friendship! It's what you needed to get you on your feet. I thought it would give you the confidence to keep going. You were close to the edge," said Steve in a quiet voice, "like I am now."

I felt myself slipping into 'amok mode'. I was so angry, so disappointed, so humiliated. I'd been living a dream. The authenticity I thought I'd found was a sham. I was a laughing stock. I was back to square one. There didn't seem to be any other squares - just circles to this one!

"But what's feeling upset?" said Steve. "It's your ego! Can't you see what you could learn from this? Haven't I taught you something? This situation is the 'Kyosaku' on your back. I've woken you up from your delusion. You were never 'empty', never 'authentic'. You were just enjoying the pretence of 'attainment'. If you had really attained something, you couldn't feel humiliated. Only egos feel humiliated, don't they?"

The carpet that's pulled from under your feet can sometimes catch you like a net, if it's pulled quickly enough. It can stop you, just before you break your spine. Steve was right, and I hated him for it. He was even a better Buddhist than me, though he didn't even pretend to be one. And how on earth does he know what a 'kyosaku' is? I bet you don't either, reader! A cascade of memories pops into my head when I'm stressed out like this.... (This is going to be another long digression. Please forgive me!)

... I never told you about this girl I knew at college. She was so easy to talk to, and we talked a lot. I bought her a coffee now and again. She probably knew that she wasn't all that horny. It's often the case that not- so-horny girls are the nicest you'll ever meet, thus proving the non-existence of God. I think Woody Allen said something like that.

She knew that I wasn't 'after her' but I could feel, almost telepathically, that she liked me. She hovered politely, not too far, not too close. Her intentions entirely honourable and respectable while my genes were just hoping for a 'smash and grab' and a quick get-a-way. I felt ashamed of myself.

One day, near Christmas, getting on for the end of term, she asked me if I wanted to come with her to a carol singing church service. I had a Christmas card in my pocket for her, but was in two minds whether or not to give it to her, in case she thought I fancied her. Yet I liked her, but couldn't, daren't convey this 'liking' because neither of us would have understood it correctly.

The 'church bit' was too much! I couldn't go through the embarrassment of it all, looking at that model of a man impaled on wood, singing boring songs, wondering whether or not I should try and get her into bed. I had to refuse. I didn't know whether it was her beliefs or her lack of horniness that stopped me making a move, but I suspected that my religious tolerance, if plotted on a scatter gram, would correlate positively with female attractiveness. Statistics is a fascinating subject! Anyway, I walked home in a depression, and I dropped her card down into the drain in the road. All this crap about 'looks don't matter'. I couldn't accept her nice little heart, her small, vulnerable, nice natured, beating little heart because I wanted big tits, white teeth behind red lips, shapely thighs and flaring hips - the type of body that doesn't crave mine - like the girl I chatted to at that psychology party. She was the high calorie pudding that I'd devour noisily, shamelessly, turning down the wholesome fruit salad and bran that had nutritional honesty.... I doubted my ability to love anyone. I could find no goodness within me. I doubted my validity as a human being, unless I was seeing the truth, that there is no love, no selflessness, that love is just another illusion.

Remember I told you about my fat friend's funeral? (How's that for gross alliteration!) I forgot to mention something really disgusting that he did. He once gathered up all the leftovers from the restaurant and put it all in a bag. He put the bag under the bonnet of his car and by the time he got home, it had been warmed up again and he sat in his car and ate the lot! Now that, to me is really foul, but I realised that this, to him, was like a frantic wank - an irresistible impulse that can't be fought against. It's like the man with the gun, running amok, mind exploded, just suffused with impulse - shooting, eating, wanking - anything to release the intolerable tension. They are equivalent things.... I tell you, I've seen into the darkness. My eyes have adjusted and I've felt my way around, carefully, feeling the walls. I've explored the darkest depth of human despair, seen it murmuring below the facade and farce of civilisation. Like the Buddha, I've seen sickness, old age and death. There are millions of people on anti-depressants in Britain! We're all going bonkers!

"Where are you going to go?" asked Steve, snapping me out of my reverie.

"I want to learn more about Buddhism, properly. I want a teacher. I want to learn about my mind. What it is, why I have one. I think Buddhists know more about the mind than any Psychologist. I'm going to have to take that risk. It might all be crap in the end but I've got nothing to lose. I have to have peace of mind now. The alternative is terrible. The alternative is unthinkable!"

Steve opened his mouth, but then closed it again. I didn't know what he was thinking. I didn't know if he agreed or disagreed. I didn't need to know.

Eventually he spoke, lighting up a joint like the pipe of peace.
"But where are you going? Tibet? Japan?"
"I had somewhere a bit nearer in mind..."

* * *

'Somewhere-or other'-shire is very much like anywhere in Britain. The train station looks like any other, so does the place where you get your taxi. When you drive through its towns, they look like any other towns. They have a W H Smith, betting shops, clothes shops, supermarkets, places that have sofas in the window with spotlights on them or plastic, corpse-like dummies with bits of their arms missing, sporting cardigans and skirts. I'm sure there's a 'Boots' and a 'MacDonald's' on one of Saturn's habitable moons.

The people don't seem much different either. No cultural variety here. No different perspective. No Red Indian mentality of peace and honour, of deep sensitivity to another's feelings- none of that. The reversed baseball cap, dark glasses and earring, mobile phone chats in the street, booming hi-fi going by in recklessly driven cars, the compulsory female tattoo on the arm, the pieces of metal through the eyebrows, (What on earth for?), the ludicrous price of beer in the pubs. 'Anywheresville' I call it. It's the place where we take our holidays in Britain. You must have been there! You know, that place that serves afternoon tea, has a museum of local historical interest, a supermarket up the road, an amusement arcade where you can watch two pence pieces hovering on the brink but never quite falling. I've been here so many times.

The taxi kept on going, into the countryside. The driver hadn't said anything since the station, but at last he chatted cheerfully.

"I like you lot," he said with a big grin, "If it wasn't for the monastery, I wouldn't make a living."

"Have you been up there, yourself? " I said.

"Me? No."

A crow was in the road ahead. It took off in good time. The sun was coming out.

"Why not? Do you think that Buddhism is crap then?"

"Don't know, mate. Not really my thing."

I fiddled with the information I had been sent and looked at the drawing of the monastery. The driver fell into another silence. He was too much of a minor character to say much and any more sentences with 'mate' in it would have made him a stereotype. The road was becoming narrower and up hill. A town lay scattered about, way below. We turned a corner and there it was, like a sandcastle at the top of a hill.

"There it is, mate," he said, "Valhalla, or whatever you call it."

"I think you've got the wrong after-life there, " I said, fishing around in my pockets for my last bit of cash.

I paid the driver and watched him disappear down the road, stirring up a cloud of dust. Soon all that could be heard was the movement of leaves in the warm breeze and the singing birds. It was blissful. No hi-fi's, no car alarms, no mobile phones ...no Off License!

I walked towards the huge wooden door of the 'sandcastle' and dropped the metal knocker. There was a very long pause before I could hear some sort of activity behind the door. It was eventually pulled open, slowly, to reveal a short man in orange robes, holding a broom. He was thin and wiry. He had a domed head with shiny, sweaty bald bits on it. (At last...somebody with a 'domed head'!) Glasses sat on his nose, catching the bright afternoon light, making him look like he had no eyes. He stood there, broom in hand, no eyes, looking at me with curiosity. I then realised that I didn't know what to say. I shrugged my shoulders and grinned.

"I come in peace...? " I suggested, foolishly.

A cloud fell across the sun and I was relieved to see that he did have eyes after all. They were brown, like a pony. He looked about fifty years old or so. But that's not important.

"Have you come to visit the monastery? " he said in a slightly high-pitched voice.

"Well yes," I said, "But I was wondering if you've got anything for restless minds..."

"How restless is it?"

"Very..."

"Show it to me."

"Show you what? " I said.

"Show me this restless mind of yours."

"I can't really. I keep it in here and it's permanently locked," I said, tapping the side of my head. It was good to talk absurdity so soon.

"Come in and have your head cut off!" He smiled and opened the door wide. What an irresistible invitation. How could I refuse?

I was led into a small room and given a booklet. The room contained things that wouldn't instantly jump to mind in a monastery. There was a large toolbox, a large collection of pots and pans, tins of paint and glue etc. All this junk was asserting itself, proclaiming their mundane reality. I knew that this was why he brought me in here first.

"We rise at four, we chant, we meditate, we have one meal before midday. We work, we meditate again and we retire at nine forty five. There is an opportunity to seek the advice of a master if you wish. You can show him your restless mind. Have you any questions?"

"I don't know much about meditation. I've just read loads of books and..."

"What do you know about meditation?"

"Just that you sit on..."

"Yes. That's it. You sit. And when sitting gets too uncomfortable, we do walking meditation to stretch our legs. We sit, we walk, we work. How does that sound?"

"What sort of work do I have to do? " I said, still wincing from that bit about four in the morning.

"There are all sorts of things that need doing. You will be able to get down to all that soon enough. You are not afraid of work are you?"

He must have come across a lot of bored, rich idiots who went into Buddhism like they'd go to Disneyland, looking for the ice cream and fun rides of enlightenment. I was better than them. I didn't come here to work though! I kept quiet.

Saturday

I've been here a week and I ache like buggery, sitting and shitting every day. It's been hard getting used to the one meal a day and my bowels are none too keen. I've swept floors and peeled potatoes too. There's no music allowed here and not much talking either. There's lots of silence that is nice for a while, then I get bored. What's wrong with a big curry and some lager, anyway?

It hasn't only been my erratic bowels that have interrupted my meditation. There is also this unpleasant sensation throughout my whole body. A shaking and shivering that goes on day and night. I don't know what it can be. I don't see this in anyone else. Sometimes I can hardly stand up it gets so bad. I think I've got the 'nausea' again. I'm trying to deny my arbitrary choice of identity. I'm trying to escape my freedom by accepting Buddhism. I'm waiting for the time when my determination will snap and I'll be back to that dreadful self that I'll never escape. Until that moment, my only refuge is in this fantasy and the hope that I'm going to find some 'truth' in all this. Their way of seeing things is still appealing to me.

To Wolfgang, (remember him?) Buddhism is totally out of the question. Not that he's actually looked into it or anything like that. No, he's found Jesus and that's that. He's decided what to believe and there can be no room for doubt. But I'd say that Jesus was a *Buddhist!* He accepted pain without protest. Suffering arose and ceased. He saw it with detachment, accepting his fate. That's what I imagine, anyway.

When I finally met my master, (known as a Roshi/I was shaking all over. It was worse in the morning. My stomach was making some very odd noises and I felt the sweat running down my back. He motioned me to sit down in front of him. I would imagine that he wouldn't appreciate it if I boffed at his feet. Not the behaviour befitting of a Bodhisattva.

'Roshi' wore robes wrapped neatly around his slim, fit frame. He looked about fifty-eight years old. An oriental, but I didn't know if he was Japanese or Chinese. He had slightly sticky-out teeth and a freckly face and bald head. His head was as smooth as an egg in its unique rolling geography. He was so 'cool' and relaxed. I envied him straight away. He was just as I had imagined a Buddhist teacher to be.

"You are an alcoholic," he pronounced with a smile. The accent was Japanese.

"Eh?"

"I can see it. You have the *delirium tremens.*"

He was looking at my hands. I held them up and saw them shaking before me, like an old man with Parkinson's disease. I don't know why I hadn't thought of that myself. It was a week since I had a drink. Perhaps I wanted to deny it.

"I know the rules," I said, feeling my own martyrdom," I'll stick with the tea."

The Roshi stood up and walked over to a small cupboard, all the while looking at me with that wise smile. He brought out a bottle of something and a glass. I watched him fill the glass and hand it to me. What kind of test was this?

"Rules are rules, but people are only human," he said.

I looked at him, dumbstruck.

"Go on..." he said.

I took his offering in two unsteady hands and brought it carefully to my mouth like the Eucharist. It was like an anvil landing on my skull! Hot metal pokers were hammered out on the anvil and forced down my throat into my stomach, glowing with flame.

"What, ... is this?" I gasped.

"Very special Japanese Saki. I believe it is good, yes?"

I nodded and coughed with gratitude. I looked up, the flames dancing within my innards, seeking an explanation. He poured me another one.

"What you want to overcome, you must first submit to," he said. I recognised it from the Tao Te Ching and never before had it seemed more appropriate. Here was a man of true compassion.

"Now, have you anything that you wish to ask me?" he said, his fingers interlocked, smiling in a teethy-sticky-out way.

"Yes. I have a lot of questions.... Can I be both Buddhist and atheist? Is Buddhism a religion? What do you actually believe? I think reincarnation is crap. Do I have to believe in it to be a Buddhist? I don't believe in any of the Buddhist legends. Are you going to kick me out for being honest? If Buddhism offers nothing after death, what is the point of it? I don't know why I've come here ... Am I looking for an identity? Does Buddhism take away all identities or does it just give people an identity that's all about not having an identity? Will it make me into something 'authentic' or is it just another way of life....I've got lots of things I want to ask you," I said. I sipped another sip of the fire. Old Roshi just looked at me, his expression exactly the same.

"Another Saki? " he said, like a mild mannered host, already pouring out the third one. I accepted it, beginning to feel pissed.

"Are there answers to these questions?" I persisted. I had waited a long time to see this man and I assumed that he was the 'boss' because he knew something most people didn't.

"It may rain later, I believe," he said.

I sensed a 'game', but I didn't want to play. I was hungry. I wanted to use the toilet again.

"Surely the questions are still there, even if we refuse to think about them or answer them. Surely there's no higher understanding by just doing nothing, just peeling damn potatoes and gardening all day long.

"What is one plus two? Answer me that."

He was trying to distract me.

"I was bad at maths at school. I actually failed the CSE exam, but I'm not that bad. " I said.

"Then you can answer me?"

"One plus two is three," I sighed, "Now, my questions..."

"Wrong! The answer is zero."

"Really? I must be worse than I thought. What did you get for maths?"

"I give you a Saki. I then give you two more. You drink them all and there are none left. Therefore one plus two is zero... Nothing."

He went on smiling, taking the mick. He was showing me that I was becoming too serious, I think. He was showing me that there are no simple answers to the simplest of questions.

"That's good! I like it," I said. "It's a good joke. But jokes aren't the truth, are they?"

"Many a truth told in jest. That's Shakespeare."

"Yes. I know! I'm not stupid! I went to university, you know."

"Knowledge isn't understanding."

"What is it that I should understand? Please make it clear to me."

"If you seek understanding, you'll never understand."

"How am I to understand without understanding?"

"I will give you a 'Koan'. A monk asked master Joshu, "Does a dog have Buddha nature? Joshu answered 'MU'. The monk was immediately enlightened. I want you to meditate on 'MU'. Come and tell me what it is when you understand. Go now...."

He pointed to the door. His face was turned away from me. I struggled to my feet, but I was dizzy with Saki. I shouldn't have been pissed though, as I'd only had three, and that much adds up to zero.

"All right. I'll do it. I'll tell you exactly what I understand it to mean..."

I meditated on 'MU'. The hours passed, although I didn't look at my watch. The DT's made meditation difficult. I decided to begin the search there. I looked for 'MU' in my churning guts, the stomach pains, the threatening need to vomit and empty my bowels, noisily. Was 'MU' here? Not if it had any sense! I looked for it in my past, my childhood, my lost teenage years. Bugger all! As I meditated, my mind wondered all over the place. It was a bit like the LSD experience. Sexual images kept haunting me. I remembered a one-night stand that so nearly happened to me. I went away for a few days with my dead, fat friend. One late evening, I went to the kitchen to get some water and the owner of the guesthouse we were staying at started to chat to me. I just wanted to go to bed and hadn't imagined that she might want anything other than a chat. She offered me a drink and I could feel this tension. It made my heart race. I don't know what stopped me making that one small effort...I like to think of it as a moral decision, since her husband was out earning money in his taxi, but I can't delude myself! I just missed it...I don't know what happened. I just missed it!

'Mu' disappeared beneath an upsurge of sexual longing and the need to relieve myself was now too much. One of the rules at this monastery is that we must not indulge in any form of sexual behaviour. That includes 'spanking the monkey'. As monkey spanking usually occurs at night between the sheets and I sleep in a dormitory with several other blokes, I have been a long while, somewhat 'lacking in spanking', if you know what I mean. It's not that I'm worried about breaking another rule....

I felt like someone with an illegal drug in his pocket as I sneaked off into the afternoon for a sunny walk and a crafty 'tug'. I soon kicked some leaves over the forensic evidence that could incriminate me if discovered. I can't believe that the celibate monks here don't do the same. There has to be a reason why the trees grow so tall here...I felt a sense of the ridiculous again, wondering why I was playing this game.

"What is 'MU'?" my master asked me at our next meeting.

"Breasts, bums, hips, thighs, silky hair, flat stomachs, bras showing through a thin...."

"Makyo'" he said, "Hallucination. Push through these images..."

"That's all I see. 'Mu' doesn't mean anything at all. You are playing a trick on me."

"Work out the trick and you'll understand 'MU'"

"I've worked it out. It's called 'Bullshit'"

"Look for the Bull. There you will find the bullshit. Then you will be so serene that you'll willingly clean your teeth with it. You can call it a Bull if you wish. We call it an Ox. It makes no difference."

"I've tried my best, but I don't think I fit in. I never fit in!"

"Stop trying. If you try to swim, you sink. If you try to sink, you float.

It's the law of inverse effort."

"I have stopped trying. I think I give up."

"Here's another riddle for you," said the master. He stood up, bowed once and then the lights went out.

I don't know what happened, but I found myself sliding down the far wall like a swatted fly. Something like a thunderbolt had struck me. I looked up from the floor in disbelief, only to see a smiling face, and arms folded neatly across orange robes.

"I hit you..." he announced with satisfaction.

"It wouldn't be rude to ask why, would it?" I gasped.

"No reason, " he said, " I just hit you."

"Is there a reason why I shouldn't hit you back? " I said, wishing I hadn't.

"You and whose army, buster?"

These were not the words and deeds I had expected from this man. Somewhere in the back of my mind I remembered that I had smugly criticised people's 'bad faith', escaping their freedom by pretending that they had to behave in determined ways. Was he showing me that that is exactly what I was doing with him? I now had contusions to add to my confusions.

"I came here to look for peace of mind," I protested, "and I find hooliganism instead!"

"I push you towards understanding. I stop your mind from working," he said.

"Several things don't seem to be working after that. My mind isn't one of them...... What did you do, anyway? That was more than a punch..."

"Kung Fu, my friend." he said, " You want any more?"

I thanked him, but declined and said I'd rather have a Saki. He poured me one and said that he was going to give me an easier Koan. I'd heard this one before. I'd heard drunk students talking about it in the bar - the one about one hand clapping. *What is the sound of one hand clapping?* He told me not to fail him, otherwise there'd be more Kung Fu.... He didn't actually say that, but I knew that's what he meant.

Tuesday

I tried very hard. Then I tried not to try, but I couldn't do that either. The urge to negate was growing stronger. Isn't meditation just sense deprivation? Aren't I putting myself in a catatonic state where I start to hallucinate? I like this place and I could so easily go along with it and accept Buddhism and allow myself some peace, but it's happening again! -The doubts, the sense of absurdity, the little boy that sees that the Emperor has nothing on. I should have kept a distance, to keep the mystery and avoid this sense of disappointment.

"What is the sound of one hand clapping? " said my master with his teethy smile.

"Masturbation, " I said. "More *slapping* than clapping, though."

"An intellectual answer. You have not broken open the riddle."

"I can't be bothered, because I know there's no correct answer..." I said. He looked at me, almost nodding.

"Zero minus two is minus two, yes?" he said.

"I see you've been brushing up on your maths."

"And zero plus two is two."

"The GCSE is in sight...."

"You are 'minus two'. Peace of mind is zero, so you must make an effort to get there, from negativity to zero. Other people are 'plus two', and they must make less effort to get to the same destination. The 'plus two's' have a better chance. They come here because they are over worked. They give too much. They try to live other people's lives as well as their own. They need rest. You think that being negative is being different, being free. You think that acceptance is conformity, reflecting of an ignorant mind. You think that the truth has to be negative. The truth isn't negative, it's zero, it's void - emptiness, pure nothingness from which everything is born and to which everything returns. You must change yourself and accept yourself before you can lose yourself..."

"I don't believe in anything. I don't think that anything is worth doing except the gratification of desires. But even these are futile. Real satisfaction always eludes me! I'm looking for something higher but can't find it in myself..."

"There is nothing high within the small minded ego - only codes and rules and conditioned responses. Good naturally flows from a state of no-mind. You cannot intellectualise about compassion. You say you don't believe in anything....You are half way there!"

"What is the rest of the way?"

"Go!"

He pointed to the door again and looked away. It was another Zen answer. You don't ask the way; you just set off. Not understanding it all is the key... I've just discovered something to motivate my 'setting off'.

Either Friday or Saturday evening....

I found a fiver in my jacket pocket! It was all crumpled up and ragged, but legal tender, sitting there in my hand, bursting with potential! It was like a fragment of the Dead Sea scrolls that held a significant prophecy. More than three 'Special Brews' could be purchased with this baby! The happiness I felt! It was embarrassing! Some time ago I had been drinking every day and not thinking anything of it. Now just a few proper drinks seemed like heaven. It proves a point, doesn't it? When we have something, we don't appreciate it. The only paradise is paradise lost!

After evening chanting, I sneaked off and made my way down the dusty track towards the town. It was a long walk but after what seemed like two thousand years, I had made it. I heard cars again. They seemed so loud! I saw women dressed to kill, walking in small groups, going to pubs and discos. They were wearing scanty summer clothes and they looked incredible. Strangely though, I didn't feel my usual frustration. I was too busy enjoying the warm evening, listening to the car alarms and police sirens from a far - the cicadas of suburbia. A large clock on the side of a building declared that it was only 8.00pm.

It didn't take me long to find an Off Licence. My hands were shaking as I picked up three cans of gold and handed the money over to the bored girl, chewing gum. She put them into a carrier bag for me and handed back a few coins of change..... I could go on like this couldn't I - giving you all these small trivial details. This seems to happen in other existentialist novels. They tell you what the main character had to eat and drink, what the weather was like and how they went for a walk and all that...But I know you'll get as bored as me unless there's some real action pretty soon. Sorry there hasn't been some sex for ages, by the way, but I hope the violence has made up for it.

I opened a can almost before I had left the premises. I gave it a good and deep slug. The taste smacked me in the face with an explosive chill of pleasure. It brought back fond memories of my half hearted suicide attempt. I sighed and wondered around the town, an outsider if ever there was one, watching people revving up for the evening. It had to be either Friday or Saturday night. There isn't this sort of anticipation on a Sunday evening, not when Monday is only hours away. Buses, trains, boredom, conflict, stress, lunch break, sandwiches, boredom, conflict, stress, buses, trains, meal, beer, bed, ad infinitum No!

This had to be a weekend- booze and riot to forget the mundane pantomime of seriousness. This is what they had been looking forward to. This is where the beer and noise and sex and release is. This is where marriages begin and break up, where children are conceived, where virginities are dispatched. Never Monday to Thursday!

Really, who needs heroin? The nine percent alcohol lager started making its journey to my skull-encased pulp of pale matter. Once there, it liberates me from the dreary rational world: " I'm in your brain, and it's just meat..." it signals back. I give it the thumbs up and smile. I don't care. I let it alter its usual chemistry, let the brown, slightly disgusting organs further down break down the potential poisons. It's all in a good cause.

I stood in front of a clothes shop, looking at the dummies, laughing at their ridiculous plastic existences. I watched people walk by, their reflections passing through the dummies, blending in with them, glass and plastic, real and reflection. I like it when things blur, when there's no certainty, no commitment to anything or any idea.

Aftershave and perfume wafted through the air as people walked by. Breasts jutting forward, declaring themselves to the world, natural, generous and abundant like ripe fruits. The girls were all laughing, sharing in some trifle, their young, warm mouths smiling, talking and laughing about nothing. Young men were walking like Gorillas, strutting their confidence, playing the game, following the mating rituals. It was too late for me to be one of them. I never had been....

I thought something was a bit odd when I once went to see 'Hawkwind' when I was sixteen. I went with my mates. I stood near the front, surrounded by people pretending to play the guitar, writhing in paroxysms of ecstasy, having seizures and convulsions to deafening sounds and blinding lights. I felt a sort of 'disgust', a 'coldness' growing within me that night. I couldn't be the joking, smoking, band- worshipping teenager any more. I was alone and I thought the band was crap. All those idiots were just at a religious ceremony, talking in tongues, receiving the Holy Spirit. It was no different to that. Their need was the same - to 'get out of yourself', out of the routine, experience something other than yourself. That 'cold' feeling wouldn't let me. It said 'No!' It said that I'll always experience reality as it is, I will have no escape from my inward turned eyes. I'll monitor all my yearnings for delusions and see them for what they are. Some time after that, I stopped listening to rock and discovered proper music! So there!

I could see the stars, above the lampposts, and a crescent moon. It's amazing to think that some men have actually walked on that thing, leaving their footprints! What a bizarre thing to do! It's like an Elephant reading 'What Hi-Fi' magazine. Unnatural, but fascinating....Hey! Wouldn't it be great to see a big photo of the surface of the moon with all the foot prints and everything and...this is the good bit....and litter! A crushed beer can, a half eaten Kebab, a puke splash! Now that would be art. You could make up your own interpretations couldn't you? Errm....Man buggers up his environment, Man's consciousness is a perfect barren wilderness but we clutter it with stupid thoughts...Who cares? It's just a good idea, isn't it?

Hey! I feel kind of 'happy' right now. I'm happy to be an outsider. I think that's what I am. It's the 'essence' I'm cramming my existence into. I don't even care that it's just 'bad faith'. I'm destined to write a modern existentialist novel and make one or two people laugh. You know, it's uncanny! A while ago, I finally got around to reading 'Hell' by Henri Barbusse. This was long after I started writing this diary, and guess how it starts! A miserable geyser alone in a room with his suitcase! But how many laughs are in that book, eh? How many laughs?

As I say, I know what I am, now. I'm an outsider. I had a go at being mentally ill, but I couldn't get on with it. Nor could Steve. Neither of us were convinced by it. Even delusions are delusion! I think I've learned to detach myself, thanks to my Buddhist 'risk'. Aggression rises and ceases, happiness rises and ceases. It has made me want to stick around and enjoy the show.

I threw the empty can into the bin by the lamppost and opened the next one. I could feel a train of thought coming on. It was leaving from platform childhood, calling at innocence, greed, manipulation, shyness, ingratitude, insecurity, inability, failure, frustration and sex. (-Please accept apologies for delay...). On through the long dark tunnel, going over the same old points, crossing too many bridges before reaching them, love (limited service due to staff shortages), loss of love and cynicism. This train will not be calling at career, cash, detached house, decent car, one-night stands and fame. For alcoholism and depression, please change at apathy. (Please remember to take all your belongings before leaving the train). Due to essential works, there will be a special bus service between existentialism and Buddhism...Please have your tickets ready for inspection.

How good it was to be pissed again! I hung about for ages, waiting for something to happen. The pubs, bowling alleys and cinemas began to fill up. There was a lot of laughter. It seemed like a good world to me. If I'd had enough money, I think I might have gone bowling myself!

Somehow I managed to stagger all the way back to the monastery. It was late, but I had no idea of the time now. My watch was in my bag. I decided a while ago that time doesn't matter and stopped wearing it. It's just a human invention anyway, just a death abacus to count away your life. It was very dark up the hill. The lampposts ran out ages ago and I didn't have a torch. Only the moon and the bright stars provided enough light to point the way - sounds a bit biblical, eh? After a while of fishing around for keys, I remembered that I hadn't any. I swore and bit my lip. I'd have to bang on the door and wake them all up. 'Knock and it shall be opened...'

After about ten minutes, I realised that no one was going to open the damned door! I took to yelling instead. They must have heard me. Someone must have woken up! I kicked the door once then hopped about, clutching my foot.

"Bastards! " I shouted, and sat down on the grass to look at the stars. They were so bright, so many millions of miles away. From what I understand, these stars may not even exist. The light that goes into my eyes has taken so long to get here that it is years and years old, and the star might have burned out by now. I might be seeing a ghost. Hey! Perhaps that's what ghosts are! - The light from a person coming across time who's dead. These lovely thoughts tumble around and across each other in a light hearted orgy. I looked at the stars and thought of infinity and eternity until something attracted my attention. There were two blue stars on the horizon, spinning pulsars getting bigger and more intense. It seemed to be a UFO or some supernatural apparition. I watched it, like pulsing plasma coming my way, throwing blue light, piercing the dark night with sheets of ectoplasm. Then a strange wailing sound, the whooping of wild animals with a ghostly echo...Suddenly, I realised that it was a bloody police car! It slowed down, headlights blazed into my face and the siren sank in tone like an opera singer, retching.

Two officers leapt out of the car and stood over me. They were massive blokes; trained, confident professionals. Reality was theirs. I had no say. What they said was right. No argument.

"Good evening sir," said one of them. He used social rules like an expert in some strange, ancient foreign custom. "We've had a complaint about a disturbance. What are you doing here, Sir?"

The blue pulsars were still spinning and aliens from another world were making contact in brief bursts of static and interference. The voices I could hear had a strange artificial tone to them, rising and falling in a way that normal people don't do.

"Are you going to take me to your planet?" I said.

"Had a drink tonight have we, sir? "

Now surely you don't expect me to make a character out of a uniformed policeman! It was dark, I'd had a lot to drink, Okay! He had a policeman's uniform on and he was wearing a hat. All I could see was a nose and I didn't note what shape it was. Sorry! His voice was a typical policeman voice that hovered between working and middle class that walked the edge of patronising and polite.

"Sshnot against shslaw, is it?"

"No, but banging on doors and shouting abuse at two in the morning *is* against the law, sir."

"This is where I'm staying. I got locked out," I explained.

"You're a Buddhist monk are you, sir?" said one of the officers in a calm and cynical tone.

"No. I'm a guest."

"You don't look like someone who belongs here, sir."

I was angry and the lights were hurting my eyes. I shielded them.

"That's stereotyping, or prejudice or sexism.... or something. I could sue you for millions," I warned.

"Would you please step into the car now, sir?"

I did not budge. I know what Steve would say. This was my inner 'child' reacting. I was defying these parental authority figures. But it's impossible to have an 'adult' to 'adult' transaction with a policeman when he has all the power and you have none. You might as well go along with the expected childish defiance.

"I'm staying here, " I said. Then I offered the suggestion that these officers had traded in their imaginations and wonder about life and the universe for the straight jacket of serious laws that have no real existence. They had no intention of discussing anarchism and philosophy with me.

"Get the cuffs on him..."

They picked me off the ground and bundled me into the car, the maniacal manacled into submission. I felt confused. Why hadn't they opened the door? Why didn't someone come and let me in? I didn't fit in. I wasn't one of them so they rejected me, turned their backs on me when their whole philosophy was supposed to be one of acceptance. They were hypocrites just like all the others!

The car started off down the track and we were soon back into the town. It was certainly a different scene to the one I had seen at eight O'clock! The pavements were littered with drunks in various stages of falling down. There was noise, abuse, ambulances, injuries, mayhem, accidents. I was just a sprat amongst the sharks and piranhas. It was a terrible sight of human suffering, but the officers were unruffled. There was the law and there was duty. They did what they did.

We pulled into the police station and I was helped out of the car and partly dragged inside. A feeling of disgrace arose then ceased. Disgrace wasn't a part of me, just a feeling, like a mist that would clear in a while. The officers behind the desk were busy. It was the routine weekend disturbances. I was checked in and then taken to a room. It was bare, smelt of fags and sweat. I was told to sit down on a chair that must have been acquainted with the bums of robbers, murderers, rapists, vandals - the lot! Shortly, a plainclothes policeman came in and sat opposite me. The jacket was from BHS, the trousers were 'Marks', the shoes from 'Clarks', but I wouldn't call his dress sense 'plain' myself. (A silly joke there. Sorry about that!)

"Had a few drinks tonight then...?" he said.

"No. None..." I said.

"I don't know why, but I find that hard to believe," he said. I smiled, warming to his sarcasm. I love sarcasm. Whoever described it as the lowest form of wit was.... oh, so *really* deep and perceptive!

"Well, you see, " I said. "First I had one Special Brew, then I had two more and that adds up to....No, hang on, I haven't got it right..."

"Piss never lies, matey. We'll have a sample from you, if you don't mind."

"Hang on...Yes! The girl in the Off License gave me a can. I drank it. That was one. Then I drank two more and that adds up to zero...Eh?"

I scratched my head and rubbed my chin. I just couldn't do the maths as that bastard Roshi had done. The man in front of me was right. Piss never lies. I was taken away into another room and handed a small bottle to produce my sample. They searched me first, just to make sure that I hadn't smuggled someone else's piss in with me to swap with mine. It wasn't too difficult to go with the flow though and I was soon holding out my sample with pride. There was truth in that piss! Good, honest, chemical truth from selfless kidneys.

"Now take him to the cells, gents," said my interrogator, "He can have the one with the four-poster and en suite."

I was led off between two policemen. They 'took me down' as they say. They asked me for my shoes and my belt, yet I could tell that they really didn't give a damn if I hanged myself or not. It was part of their job, to make society run efficiently. Scratch into its chest of laws and you'll find accountability instead of a heart.

"Sleep it off, sunshine. Good night," they said, and left me behind a door that wouldn't look out of place in a decompression chamber or a bank vault. The interior, however, wasn't very different from the Spartan monastery accommodation, except for the privacy I had now acquired. I lay back on the hard 'bed' and looked up at the ceiling, just before the lights went out. My freedom had been taken away from me, and it felt good. I had no choices and no decisions to make. Others were controlling me for now. I could get used to this! I was their puppet in the making. I'd be classified, priced, labelled, and processed. I was Pinocchio handing in his strings to become a block of wood again. I pretended I was Meursault, awaiting the guillotine the next morning, basking in the "...benign indifference of the world..."

The sounds of hell, of sick, tortured minds boomed around the metallic cells. There were incoherent challenges to violence, insults and threats that nobody heard or could respond to. These voices were just fists waving at the clouds. It will all soon give way to sleep, to blissful unconsciousness, and one day, there'll be no hangover.

Next day

But not this morning! That thumping noise was coming from my head and that faint red glow was the sunrise of a psychosis.

I was shown into the same room as yesterday and given a cup of tea. This time a fairly bulky man in a suit slightly too big for him sat opposite me and started filling out some forms, very rapidly. He had obviously done this many times before. Eventually he looked up at me, slightly weary, slightly judgemental.

"This appears to be your first offence. We've found nothing else on you. Why were you trying to get into that monastery? " he said, clicking his 'biro'.

"I was locked out. I was a guest there. I told them last night."

He stared at me. There was nothing you could read in his face. He'd seen it all; human stupidity and depravity. He was immune to it.

"The complainant denies that you are a guest there. We've just been speaking to the head monk. We gave him your name and he's never heard of you. What do you say to that?"

I stared at the table, examining its coffee stains and cigarette scorch marks. The surface loomed up at me, like Bertrand Russell's table. Nothing was certain or predictable. Reality distorted, moving in and out of focus, gently dancing with my sweet need for vengeance. The strange 'cold' feeling again, like at the 'Hawkwind' concert, like when that horse-like woman ditched me then pulled away all my hopes. My life was a parade of betrayal and it was now pay back time!

"We've turned up a history of mental problems; a stay in psychiatric hospital. A doctor ...Steve Smith has confirmed that you have a rather loose grip on reality. You've also used LSD..."

"Steve said that? " I said in a quiet whisper.

"You've got to get yourself sorted out, mate. Get a job before you get yourself into some serious trouble. I'll give you a break. I'm letting you off with a caution. You can go now, but keep out of trouble. You understand?"

I looked up. I must have looked ashen.

"I can tell you the name of the monks and the guests. I *was* staying there. I've been betrayed."

He pointed a fat finger at me and shook his head.

"Don't push it!" he said. "I can still put you on a charge. Get your stuff and get out before I change my mind!"

I left the station with a handful of loose change, an empty stomach and an unstoppable desire for revenge. That old 'Roshi' had made a complete fool out of me, toying with me for his own amusement, then locking me out because I wasn't like his other conforming, ingratiating little 'yes men'. I had failed at being a Buddhist too and I had been rejected from even this - a philosophy that is all about acceptance of everything and everyone. The hypocrites! The arrogance! There was only one thing left to do. Raskolinikov bludgeoned a stupid old bag to death, Meursault shot an Arab and couldn't give a shit about what he'd done, and I....I shall fulfil my mission to be a character in an existentialist novel. I shall give way to my emotion to run amok, at last. It is good. It needs to be done. I will take care of him then I'll go back for Steve.

Hatred, so pure and powerful, like love played backwards, it filled my being. It was like a nuclear reactor out of control, going into meltdown. Nothing could stop the process now, no reasoning, no rationality. Sex, money, fame - all trifles cast into the inferno, the flames now causing the edges of my personality to twist and buckle. Two eyes stared ahead; two legs moved mechanically forward like Frankenstein's monster. The axe in the gardens glinted in my mind, as sharp as the tool itself. So much for police efficiency! There was going to be a murder within half an hour of a caution. Someone would be blamed, someone would pass the buck, someone would write a report and someone would say: "We must make sure that this never happens again." Then we'd be forgotten, the murderer and murdered, forgotten and it'll be business as usual.

It was a lovely day to kill someone. My hangover was clearing, as clear as my mind and my purpose. Morality, ethics, compassion, social rules, they could all be transcended, not just by lunatics, but by everyone. We are held together by bits of glue and string. You only have to look to see it. Let him who has eyes to see, open them if you dare! We have the same morality as conditioned rats, pulling levers for God's favour or social approval. All you charity workers, you smug 'good people' who raise money for your egos and your self congratulatory social conscience, all you 'nice' people who help others - damn you all! There is no 'good' and you're all going to die, like me, like old Roshi and you'll be forgotten, cast into the abyss of time! The coffin awaits you and your good intentions and there'll just be the smiling worms or the orange flames to greet you. But I am going to make an impact! I'm going to make a difference now. I'm going to show you that

I won't accept indifference any longer! I'll show you that I can fight back! Fight back from rejection!

I made my way up the track and sneaked my way around the back of the building, into the gardens. There was nobody about. I could hear chanting from inside. There were no axes immediately to hand so I went into the storage shed and found one there - a heavy machete. It felt balanced and poised for action in my hand. I felt so alive and free! This was going to be my definitive moment, making life worthwhile after all. I hid behind the shed and waited for the Roshi to come out...

After the chanting, he appeared. His hands were folded across his chest. He was slowly walking towards the wooded area where I 'spanked the monkey'. If he was going there for the same reason and I had a camera, I would spare his life. His total humiliation would be even better. That dignified expression, those wise words, those Zen puzzles would suddenly evaporate with just one picture of him 'twanging the wire' like everyone else. Oh what a great leveller masturbation is! How it tears down our pathetic poses!

I crept slowly after him, acquiring the agility and silence of a cat. I was back to my roots. I had an enemy that I was stalking. My adrenalin was pumping. I was channelling my hatred like fuel into my efficient engine of movement. He was going to feel fear, and to show me fear. I was going to watch his pathetic collection of ideas and poses melt on his face. He was going to see how his silly Kung Fu was just an executive toy compared to the heavy brutality of a machete. He was going to see his own hypocrisy staring back at him, naked and trembling...

He suddenly turned around, hearing me behind him. It was the classic foot snapping the twig cliché, but it was perfectly timed. He looked at me and then at the axe and smiled. Perhaps he had not quite got it! Perhaps he thought that I'd come to gather firewood or something. I had to make my intentions clear. It was a great scene, like a Western. I was Clint Eastwood. I had to have a calm, quiet, gritty voice. I wish I had been wearing a hat, just over my eyes. I would have a shadow trailing behind me, and there'd be music by Ennio Moriconne....

"I've got a Koan for you, " I said. " If my Master is hacked to death in a forest and no-one hears his screams, does he make a sound?"

Do you know what he did? Can you even guess? He bowed slowly then placed his neck on a tree stump, like a chopping block, carefully pulling the top of his robe back to expose the target. There wasn't the slightest fear, not the slightest! And the anger, the revenge, the betrayal, the humiliation....they all slipped from me and I understood without understanding. It was over. Everything became transparent and clear. There was no need for words; it was all obvious. I dropped slowly to my knees, like a deflated balloon. There was nothing left. Not the slightest burden. There was just a vacuum, and into the vacuum flooded trees and stars, animals, people, plants and planets. I was everything and everything was me. That's why all my characters are the same. We are all the same person in different guises.

Old Roshi eventually adjusted his robes and stood up. He looked down at me, smiling.

"You dropped your axe," he said. Still on my knees, I looked at him, vacantly.

"I dropped it. I dropped..."

"Leave it where it has fallen," he said.

I continued staring at his fearless, ridiculous face.

"I hear it," I said. " I hear the sound. I know the sound of one hand clapping... The performance *is* the applause. The applause *is* the performance. It's *one* thing! There's no separation! There isn't *life* and then our awareness of it. There's only life..."

He bowed.

"Now show me 'MU'," he said.

"It is here!" I said, without hesitation. He bowed again and nodded. He had come so close to nodding in the manner of several of Henry VIII wives.

We walked slowly back inside. He said that he had something for me. I thought it might have been a Saki, but he gave me some orange robes. I took them and bowed.

"It is windy today," he said.

"The vegetables need it," I replied.

He bowed and the gong for the meal rang.

* * *

...And if you believe that, you'll believe anything!

Epilogue

The universe is a park bench and we are just the vagrants passing through. Beer and fags, our empathy and compassion are all we have. Before the police move us on, before the authorities make us get a job; before our employers, our religions, our societies fit us up with a suit and a matching mask – if we are lucky enough, we can look at our shabby clothes and see with clear eyes that we have nothing – no identity, just flesh and bone that we cover with an overcoat fished out the bin of our culture – something that once belonged to someone else, something to cover our shame. In that recognition, our search begins – from alienation to ataraxia – and ends at the same time.

Moli
a
Meg

mynd am dro ... i'r sinema

Christa Richardson

© CAA Cymru 2020
CAA Cymru – un o frandiau Atebol

Argraffwyd yn wreiddiol yn 2018
Argraffwyd yr argraffiad newydd cyntaf yn 2020
Ail argraffwyd yn 2021

Cyhoeddwyd yng Nghymru yn 2021 gan CAA Cymru, Adeiladau'r Fagwyr,
Llanfihangel Genau'r Glyn, Aberystwyth, Ceredigion SY24 5AQ

Ariennir yn rhannol gan Lywodraeth Cymru fel rhan o'i rhaglen gomisiynu
adnoddau addysgu a dysgu Cymraeg a dwyieithog

Argraffwyd a rhwymwyd yng Nghymru gan Argraffwyr Cambria, Aberystwyth

ISBN: 978-1-84521-633-7

Mae cofnod catalog ar gyfer y cyhoeddiad hwn ar gael yn Llyfrgell Genedlaethol
Cymru a'r Llyfrgell Brydeinig

Cydnabyddiaethau
Diolch i Sarah Davies, Chloe Edwards, Siân Pryce Edwards a Sharon Jones am
eu harweiniad gwerthfawr

www.atebol.com

Dyma Moli.

Dyma Meg.

Mae Moli a Meg yn ffrindiau da.

Mae Moli a Meg
yn mynd i'r sinema.

4

Mae Meg yn prynu
dau docyn.
Un i Moli. Un i Meg.

Mae Moli yn prynu popcorn.
Un i Meg. Un i Moli.

Mae Moli a Meg yn gwylio'r ffilm.

Mae Moli a Meg yn
bwyta'r popcorn.
Mmm! Blasus iawn!

Mae Moli a Meg
yn hoffi mynd
i'r sinema.

9

Hwyl fawr, Moli!
Hwyl fawr, Meg!